EBURY PRESS

ALL HE LEFT ME WAS A RECIPE

Shenaz Treasury, India's OG MTV VJ and Bollywood's charismatic 'it' girl from *Ishq Vishk* and *Delhi Belly*, has become India's hottest travel vlogger. A dynamic entertainer, Shenaz has moved beyond acting over the years. She wrote, produced and hosted *Culture Shock* for Discovery Travel Channel, US, and sold a screenplay to Yash Raj.

In the US, Shenaz acted in 107 episodes of *One Life to Live* on ABC and added her humour to *The Nightly Show* on Comedy Central, produced by Jon Stewart. She played a memorable role in the Oscar-nominated *The Big Sick*, produced by Judd Apatow, and starred in *Brown Nation* on Netflix.

Back in India, Shenaz reigns as the country's top travel vlogger. Her debut book, *All He Left Me Was a Recipe*, ventures into relationship dramas, aiming for an exciting web series adaptation.

Celebrating 35 Years of
Penguin Random House India

All He Left Me Was a Recipe

LESSONS FROM MY BREAK-UPS

SHENAZ TREASURY

EBURY
PRESS

An imprint of Penguin Random House

EBURY PRESS

USA | Canada | UK | Ireland | Australia
New Zealand | India | South Africa | China | Singapore

Ebury Press is part of the Penguin Random House group of companies
whose addresses can be found at global.penguinrandomhouse.com

Published by Penguin Random House India Pvt. Ltd
4th Floor, Capital Tower 1, MG Road,
Gurugram 122 002, Haryana, India

First published in Ebury Press by Penguin Random House India 2023

Illustrations by Parthika Immaneni

10 9 8 7 6 5 4 3 2 1

ISBN 9780143441212

Typeset in Sabon by Manipal Technologies Limited, Manipal

www.penguin.co.in

So what is this book about?

If there is anything we all have experienced, it's a break-up.

Some more than others.

I belong in the category that has experienced more break-ups than most people.

How many?

Lost count, long ago!

That makes me a break-up expert (you would think).

Yet, I am the worst 'break-upper'.

The more break-ups I have, the harder it gets

Every break-up hurts a little bit more.

So I decided to write this book to celebrate break-ups!

Mine, yours and everyone's!

This book has been written to remind you and me that there is always a next chapter!

The way I see it is that the beginnings are just for Bollywood movies, Disney dramas and Instagram couples.

All our real-life love stories have more than just a beginning.

We have a middle and most times an end.

We usually celebrate the beginning, sleepwalk our way to the middle and procrastinate the end.

We never really romanticize or celebrate the end. We are scared of it. We look at it as the worst period in our lives. Yet our endings make us who we are.

All our life lessons or recipes come from the endings and not beginnings.

Each chapter is:

A new guy or the same guy at a different time.

Another promise.

A unique adventure.

A different ending.

A special recipe.

And:

A lesson learnt.

What's fact? What's fiction?

The fact part is the trajectory of my life.

I was the baby on the ship, grew up in Bandra, Mumbai, lived in Singapore, Hong Kong, Bangkok, New York, Los Angeles and then back in Mumbai.

Worked at MTV, acted in movies, Bollywood movies, Hollywood shows, wrote a screenplay, became a content creator and now an author.

All this is TRUE!

You must write from what you know, right?

So, I've let the protagonist have my life.

The fiction/fantasy part include some of the boys.

And some of the incidents.

They may seem real.

But that may be because you recognize these guys or incidents as part of your life.

At least, I hope you do.

That would mean I have done a good job.

All right then,

Thanks!

Hope you enjoy the book and gift it to your friends, especially the ones who are looking for love, going through a break-up or stuck in a challenging relationship.

1

WHAT ARE THE RULES OF BREAK-UP?

It all started when she was three years old.

She lived on a ship, a huge cargo ship that sailed the world. Like *Life of Pi* without the animals.

Her company: a bunch of potty mouth sailors from all over the world.

Her food: canned sausages. And if they were lucky, some eggs. Vegetables were a delicacy that they only got when their ship docked somewhere. And being on land was a weird, unnatural thing that she spent hours fantasizing about.

All she knew was the ocean. The ship was her city, the cabin her home. She didn't know kids her age or a home that didn't move from continent to continent.

Her parents passed their time in the evenings playing scrabble and table tennis while she watched quietly. 'Children are meant to be seen, not heard', was what the sailors told her. So, she spoke very little.

She was a Captain Spock baby, not the *Star Trek* Spock with the ears but the paediatrician Spock from Connecticut who advocated 'when babies cry, adults should put on earplugs'.

She spent her endless time speaking to imaginary mermaids, fishing with a fishing rod that did not reach the ocean and dreaming about what it would be like to live on land as she stared into the horizon and watched the sun disappear into the sea every evening.

There were no other little people on board. In fact, she had never played with another child her age.

Then, one day, their ship docked in Mayagüez, Puerto Rico.

Her parents took her to a park and she slurped from a giant watermelon while she sat on the swing staring at trees. Trees that stood in one place and never moved. She wondered what it would be like to be a tree, rooted in one place.

A three-year-old boy, wearing diapers and nothing else, entered the park with his parents. He had a brown curly fro, his skin was sun-kissed, he had a bright black birthmark on his cheek and a giant toothless grin. She could tell he had a nice booty, even though he had diapers on.

It was love at first sight for her.

She dropped her watermelon to the ground and sat there drinking Nappy Boy in. He looked tastier than her milk-bottle.

He must have caught her staring. He smiled and threw a ball at her and that was the moment she felt her heart skip a beat for the first time. She smiled at him widely, ignoring the ball.

Nappy Boy looked at her toothless grin wide-eyed. Terrified, he started to run.

She didn't read the signs.

She jumped out of the swing and ran towards him with a huge watermelon-stained smile. He screamed and scuttled away.

She threw herself on him, sticking her tongue out, and tried licking the birthmark on his face. It looked like a chocolate M&M.

He shrieked.

WHAM! Something hit her across her forehead. It was her fallen watermelon.

She fell flat on the ground, seeing stars.

When she woke up, he was gone. She cried and cried.

Her first break-up.

Needless to say, all her relationships with the opposite sex followed that very pattern. And every time she looks at a watermelon she thinks about her first love in Mayagüez, Puerto Rico.

RECIPE

Watermelon. Cut
in two halves.

LESSON LEARNT

Boys can hurt.

NOTHING is fair in
love and break-ups.

Boys are like mashed
bananas—sweet and
delightful, but they
might just leave you
with a messy bib.

WHERE IS HE NOW?

She never encountered the boy again.

2

IS ATTRACTION MORE THAN JUST LOOKS?

S he was fourteen when she got her first period.

'Mom I'm bleeding!' she announced loudly as her family was having a party.

'This is such great news,' her aunties said overjoyed, 'we must celebrate.'

They stuffed their faces with cake and wafers as they congratulated her. She walked with her legs apart, wondering if she would die of humiliation or disgust from the blood coming out of her 'private part'.

Big hair, big teeth, big calves, big lips—she was the poster girl for big and awkward.

Dropped into the world of rich, bratty privileged girls of Baha Bai Petit, a posh school in Bandra, she forced her dad to park his fat, rundown Ambassador far from the school gate so nobody would see her getting out from it. She sat in the bell tower in the lunch break so nobody could see she had no friends. She missed her fishing rod, the non-judgemental ocean. She imagined her mermaid friends missed her. She day-dreamed a lot.

She noticed her changing body for the first time when Ameesha Sippy, a classmate, asked her if her thighs rubbed in front of a herd of other classmates. They all laughed and pointed at her 'thunder thighs'.

And so, the body shaming began.

To add to her misery, a culex mosquito bit her, and for a whole year, she had something that made her left leg really, really large—like a tree trunk. The doctor called it elephantiasis (perfect!) and promised it would go away. She woke up every day, looked at her legs, screamed and begged not to go to school. She rubbed onions in her armpits because she had heard a rumour that it gave you the flu but it didn't work. She was in school every day, pulling her skirt down, trying to hide her legs.

So, when in class 9, she suddenly started getting an anonymous call from a stranger on her landline, she did not hang up.

The voice on the other end of the phone said he saw her walking to her house every day in her school uniform from her tuitions. He said she was pretty.

She waited for his call every day. He was her only friend. She shared imaginary stories and what her life on the ship was like with him. Soon, not a day went by when she did not speak to him. She would wait till her parents were out and the coast was clear to call him. They talked into the night. If her parents picked up the extension, she hung up. If he called and her parents picked up, he hung up.

Then, nine months later, after much coaxing, she agreed to meet him. She told her parents she was going to her friend Kanika's house, who lived in Versova (considered the end of the world from Bandra at that time). She waited on a street corner of Andheri for a red Maruti van, as per his 'instructions'.

Her hands were trembling. *What if I lose my voice and no words come out? What if my hands don't stop shaking? What if he notices my elephant leg and drives off? What if he realizes I am not pretty after all? What if . . .*

A red Maruti van screeched to a halt on the curb. She got in nervously. She didn't even look up until he started driving.

Finally, she peered through her bangs at him. She almost choked. He looked a lot older than her fourteen -year-old self. He stared her down with eyes that seemed to pop out of his head.

He wasn't like Joe Hardy from *Hardy Boys* or Ned from the *Nancy Drew* books that she had imagined him to be. This was DEFINITELY NOT LOVE AT FIRST SIGHT. She flinched.

But she had spoken to him for months and couldn't bail now. Oh no. She was stuck. This was her future husband. Their kids would have bulgy eyes, elephant legs and bangs.

And so began her romance with the bulgy eyed boy. He was three years older than her and could even ride a motor bike. They went to movies, sat on the rocks on Bandstand and rode around on his bike. The whole time she felt she should tell him that she had changed her mind about their relationship.

But when she listened to Def Leppard while he lay next to her with all their clothes on and wolfed down the biryani at his home and hugged his mother warmly, she thought why not? Never had she eaten biryani like this. His mom would usher her into the kitchen while she layered the rice. She'd watch eagerly. She was even part of their Eid celebration.

And when they meandered through Versova on his motorbike, she felt like Ameesha Sippy and the other sexy girls in her class. She felt good; for the first time in her life she had a real friend. His bulgy eyes didn't look bulgy anymore, she found them endearing.

And his smile, it was like a glimmer of hope.

His voice was so calming like a melody in a storm.

She scribbled in her diary, 'Am I falling for the boy with the bulgy eyes? Could love not be about looks but about how he wipes your tears when you are down? Could love be about how he supports your hopes and dreams and listens intently to all your stories? Could love be the way he loves you—flaws and all?'

He told her he loved her face, her arms, her legs and even kissed her swollen 'elephantiasis'-ed ankles. The boy with bulgy eyes made her feel like a beauty queen. She started loving his eyes that twinkled every time he looked at her. And she wondered, 'Do you fall in love with people who are in love with you?' The bulgy eyed boy made her smile.

In those moments she forgot about Ameesha Sippy and the mean girls. His eyes didn't seem to pop anymore; she grew to love his smile and his crooked teeth.

Then one day, on 15 August, she bunked her French tuition to watch a James Bond film—*Tomorrow Never Dies*—with him. As the movie let out, they walked out hand in hand, laughing, exhilarated from all the race car driving.

He suddenly went white and said, 'Your dad.'

She didn't believe him.

'Shut up, stop lying,' she laughed.

'No really, it's your dad.'

She turned and her dad almost lifted her up in anger. She stared at him. She had been caught red-handed with the boy with the bulgy eyes.

She turned to him. 'RUN,' she said but realized she didn't need to even say it, he had already sprinted off. Her dad pushed her into his Ambassador and drove like a rickshaw driver on top of pavements, chasing the boy with the bulgy eyes. The boy ran through markets

and pedestrians, through cows grazing on trash but her
dad, in James Bond mode, was not going to let him get
away. Beep Beep Beep . . .

Her dad, who usually never honked, beeped loudly
as a stray goat lazily crossed in front of their car. They
almost hit it but all she could think about was mutton
biryani! Would she never eat his mom's biryani again?

Finally their Ambassador caught up with the boy
with the bulgy eyes. Her dad yelled, 'You! You! What are
you doing with my daughter? What were you doing with
her in the dark in the theatre?'

She stared at the boy wide eyed. *Was he going to ask
for my hand in marriage? Was he going to go down on
his knees? Was he going to . . .*

The boy with the bulgy eyes gulped and muttered,
'I don't know your daughter, Sir. Never seen her in my life.'

Her dad gave him a hard stare. 'If I ever see you with
my daughter, I will take you to the police.'

And that was it. That was the last she ever saw
of him.

Every 15 August from that day, she bit her lips and
hung her head in shame in front of her parents. And when
the phone rang, she did not pick it up.

The boy with the bulgy eyes left her with a love for
Def Leppard and an obsession with biryani. But the best
gift he left her with was a big bag full of confidence.

Recipe:

Mutton biryani

LESSON LEARNT

1. It's not how he looks,
   it's how he makes
   you feel.

2. Some boys can be
   like chole bhature,
   not the most visually
   appealing at first but
   they will fill your soul
   with comfort and joy.

WHERE IS HE NOW?

She met him at a movie theatre
recently. They exchanged
pleasantries. She walked away
with a warm feeling, hoping he
was happy in life.

Three Thank You's and a Sorry:

1. She thanks him for making her feel like a swan when her school friends made her feel like the ugly duckling.

2. She thanks him for the bike rides from Bandra to Versova.

3. She thanks him for introducing her to rock music.

She is sorry she judged him for the way he looked.

She Misses:

1. The freedom she felt at the back of his bike.

2. His bulgy eyes.

3. The long phone conversations.

3

Is One-Sided Love Real?

At age fifteen, she found herself packing up all her George Michael posters and moving from Hill Road to Turner Road in Bandra, Mumbai, so her parents could take care of Silu Granny, her father's mother.

Silu Granny was four feet nine inches tall. She was tiny but all muscle, with a surprisingly hot bod for a woman her age. She had an eyepatch because of a cataract operation. She never removed it, so she basically looked like a hot pirate at seventy-nine.

She shifted around in old lady shoes, and you could always hear her coming. Don't be fooled; she saw everything, even if it was only with one eye.

Silu Granny was very proud of her petite figure, especially her toned muscular legs. She told stories about how men talked about her legs back in the 1950s. She still wore shorter skirts than most grandmothers which embarrassed her sister but delighted her.

She went on crash diets. 'Only fruit for me today; I can't afford to gain weight,' she would exclaim at the hint of a belly.

Granny loved *The Bold and the Beautiful* that aired at 11.30 a.m. every day. Whatever happened, Granny had to watch *The Bold and the Beautiful.*

Granny was obsessed with water. The bathroom was always full of buckets of water, and even though everyone tried to convince her that they had no water shortage, she refused to listen.

Granny refused to take cabs and always took the train or bus even in the dead of night.

And then she would put a rupee in the weighing scale at the station and check her weight. If it was above what she wanted, the whole family had to skip dinner that night. So, everyone always hid the coins.

She was ruthless and afraid of NOTHING!

Except . . . except . . . this one particular crow that sat on her window every day. You see, in India we believe that crows are our ancestors. She was convinced the crow was her dead husband and that he was angry at her.

Granny and Grandpa's love story was simple and delightful, like those of most people in the 1950s. Pre-Tinder, pre-Bumble, pre-Instagram.

They lived across the road from each other. Grandpa stared into her window, she stared back, and they fell in love and got married.

There were stories about Grandpa. He was a gallant man, a true gentleman. He would put Grandma in a cab and run after it from Bandra to Colaba just to see that she was home safe. He was the first person in his neighbourhood to have a phone at home and women came from everywhere to use it, but he had eyes only for Silu Granny and her short skirts.

She didn't know this side of Grandpa. She had only seen him in a wheelchair, with Parkinson's. It made her sad. He was gone now. But she saw pictures of him, when he was young and stood tall, always a gentleman, always soft-spoken. He loved Granny and she loved him.

But Granny had some guilt. Maybe it was about not letting him eat ice cream just a few days before he passed away, maybe it was something else.

Granny insisted he was back in the form of a very enraged crow, sitting on her head every time she went outside.

Granny (running inside) would say, 'He sat on my head again. He is angry.'

Granny loved cutlets (Parsi cutlets). She would get them from Britannia, the oldest Parsi restaurant in Mumbai, and save them in the fridge with a note attached to a toothpick that said, 'DO NOT EAT, THIS IS GRANNY'S.'

But she was sixteen and she was hungry. She would sometimes eat all her grandmother's cutlets. Granny would be very disappointed in her but later would forgive her after giving her a good scolding. She wouldn't forgive her sister though.

See, the girl was Granny's favourite. For some reason, she and Granny had a special kinship. She admired

Granny. To her, Granny was like a pirate grandmom with an eyepatch, sexy legs and a killer attitude.

When she was sick, her granny would sit at the edge of her bed on a stool and pet her head until she fell asleep.

When her parents went out of town, she locked Granny in her room and had parties in the big house. But Granny always escaped. She'd wander into the room with her pirate eyepatch and above-the-knee dresses (very edgy for a woman her age) and her friends would gasp in shock.

'Who is that??' She would then escort her granny to her room and lock her up again.

But Granny never ratted her out to her parents. Her sister would, but Granny would not even speak of it. Maybe she forgot, maybe it was their little secret.

By the time she turned sixteen, she was in love with a boy. He would ride by Vina Villa on his bike. He was a tall Anglo-Indian with a prominent jaw, jet black hair and sexy stubble. To Granny, he looked like Ridge Forester from *The Bold and the Beautiful*. But to her, he looked like Johnny from *Dirty Dancing*. Granny would catch her watching him and give her an approving nod. *Could Granny see him with one eye?*

Dirty Dancing Dude was her senior at Xavier's.

Every time he would enter the college canteen, a hush would come over. Dirty Dancing Dude is here! The entire college, boys and girls in unison, would turn around to look at him.

Dirty Dancing Dude would walk in slo-mo with a sexy, confident swagger. He'd take out a cigarette and effortlessly flick it into his mouth (like Travolta in *Grease*).

Dirty Dancing Dude had an aura and charisma that would make it appear as though the world around him was frozen in time.

At first a few boys and girls, then the entire canteen started to follow Dirty Dancing Dude as if he were the Pied Piper. She was one of many who trailed him, caught under his magical spell.

Ameesha Sippy (yes, she followed her to Xavier's) pushed her aside, causing her to stumble and fall. But the crowd just stepped over and past her, continuing to blindly follow him.

She didn't care; she just looked up at him strutting away in the distance, tears of love welling up in her eyes. She didn't stand a chance.

Then, one day, he was sitting under a tree in the centre of a group of swooning girls. He was playing the guitar and singing softly, almost to himself. She peered into the circle. They made eye contact. She shivered.

'Hey, check this out. My cousin Ryan just got back from America and brought me this,' he said to all the girls as he reached into his backpack and pulled out a CD. It was the soundtrack to *Dirty Dancing* with Patrick Swayze manhandling Jennifer Grey on the cover.

'This is what everyone in America is listening to right now.'

All the girls ooh-ed and ahhh-ed! He then reached into his backpack and slowly pulled out a fat, blocky contraption.

'It's called a Discman.' All the girls went 'Oh my God . . . imported!' The girls moved in to have a closer look. Ameesha Sippy stepped on her toe.

'Move fatty!' she yelled loudly at her. Embarrassed, she scurried away.

But then, one fine day, she decided it was time to make her move. She spotted him talking to a small group of self-consciously cool guys. She walked boldly up to them.

On her approach, she noticed the *Dirty Dancing* CD sticking out from the elastic meshing on his backpack.

She stopped just behind him and slowly reached out in an attempt to tap his shoulder. But she lacked the courage. Instead, she secretly snatched the CD from his backpack and quickly ran away. No one noticed.

Their romance had begun.

She put the phone receiver up against the speakers of an old model CD player and pressed play. 'Hungry Eyes' filled the room.

'Hello? Are you the girl who stole my CD? Hello? Hello?' He didn't hang up. He seemed to find this amusing.

She called him every day after that and played songs from the CD to him. She'd imagine him shirtless, painting a large canvass with a brush tucked under his ear.

When she told her friend Gunjeet about it, she couldn't believe her ears.

'You call and play music for him?' she asked disbelievingly.

'Yes, it's part of my plan. I've broken it down into phases, see. Phase one is to soften him up with songs. Phase two, I'll . . .

'There's a much simpler way,' said Gunjeet cutting her short.

She picked up the rotary phone receiver and dialled. No! NO! NO! she tried to stop her.

She was hyperventilating.

'You're jumping to phase five!'

Gunjeet held up her hand and listened to his phone ringing on the other end.

'Hi, it's Gunjeet. Gunjeet Marwah from Chemistry. Thank you! Yes, I just had my hair cut . . .'

Gunjeet flipped her hair back flirtatiously.

'What the hell!' she whispered. 'Stop flirting with him. He's mine!' She waved her hands wildly, about to combust.

'So, anyway, the reason I called was I wanted to ask you something.'

She listened, blushing.

'Oh, you're too sweet . . . Thank you. I do have a personal trainer, yes . . .'

She turned red. 'Gunjeet! Gunjeet!'

'So, um, what do you think of my friend?'

She yelped, covering her mouth and moved in to share the receiver with Gunjeet.

'Who? Oh, oh oh you mean Buffalo Butt?' he asked.

Her face fell. Thunder sounded. Lightning struck! The ceiling crumbled and collapsed on top of her head.

She sat in the middle of a cloud of dust and particles, completely covered in dirt and dried plaster.

Behind the dust and dirt, her eyes slowly welled up with tears.

Gunjeet laughed. 'Guess you need to lose weight, Buffalo Butt,' she said. Then she left, flicking her hair. She was one of those friends who made you feel bad about yourself and then left. That night, she cried herself to sleep. Silu Granny knocked on the door. Granny offered her a CUTLET! She refused.

And that was how her manic obsession with weight loss began.

Granny and she went on many diets together. The all-bread diet, which didn't work out. The all-almond diet, after which she had to get her stomach pumped from protein poisoning. The all-papaya diet that kept her in the bathroom all day.

She started taking classes.

Aerobic class: She kicked her leg out of sync with the rest of the class. She came home and Silu Granny hugged her.

Khar Gym Swimming Pool: She swam laps past screaming kids. Under water she saw a yellow liquid surrounding the kids. She made a face, held her breath and swam through it. She came home and Silu Granny had hot water in a bucket waiting for her in the bathroom.

Boxing Ring: She trained, kicking feverishly at a pad held up by a kick-boxing coach. Then she slipped, missed the pad and nailed the coach between the legs. He fell to the floor in pain. She came home with a headache and Granny patted her to sleep.

Three months later, she checked out her butt in front of the mirror, pleased with herself.

But she could never stop the binging, which became worse every time she thought of Dirty Dancing Dude.

His voice kept echoing in her head. *Buffalo Butt . . . Buffalo Butt . . . Buffalo Butt . . .* She reached for Granny's cutlet, shoving the whole thing into her mouth. Granny frowned at her. THAT'S MINE!

Six months later, he moved to New York City. Since then, she had one wish. *I will go to New York City. We will meet at Times Square outside Mc Donald's; he will see my slim butt in black pants, tell me I look thin and beautiful. And we will be in love.*

RECIPE:

*Parsi Mutton Cutlet
from Britannia's with a
toothpick on top saying
'DO NOT EAT'*

LESSON LEARNT

1. *Infatuation is like a velvety crème brûlée that sends your taste buds into a frenzy.*

2. *Granny was her best friend.*

3. *Best friends come in different shapes, forms and ages.*

4. *There are some girls who are there to just make you feel worse about yourself.*

5. *These mean girls have mastered the art of snide remarks and backhanded compliments. They can make you feel like a wilted salad on a cloudy day.*

4

COULD A BOY BE THREATENED BY A GIRL'S SUCCESS?

*P*retty *Woman* came out in Regal Cinema in the 1990s and ran for a year. She went to see the movie with a cute chubby boy from Hill Road. During the interval, as they fed each other butter popcorn, someone, who unfortunately wasn't Richard Gere, pulled her aside and asked her to go upstairs where a photoshoot was in progress. There were ten other girls up there. They took her pictures and sent her home. Six months later, she got a call saying she had won the Pretty Woman Contest in India. She didn't even know she had taken part in it but was thrilled because the prize was a modelling contract for a store called Pink Panther in Bandra and they would give her clothes worth Rs 5000 from the store. She was over the moon! *Clothes from Pink Panther! What else could a sixteen-year-old girl ask for? All the diets were finally paying off!*

So far, she had been cutting up her mom's clothes from the 1970s and trying to look like Gwen Stefani of the 1990s. One top every three months from Fashion Street was all she could afford on her pocket money. Pink Panther was Versace for her sixteen-year-old self. She was determined to not mess this up.

The shoot clashed with a trip that her dad had booked for the family in Goa.

'The hotel I've booked costs much more than Rs 5000. Experiences matter more than clothes,' lamented Dad.

'But this will be an experience.'

She begged and pleaded and finally her parents agreed to leave her behind in Bombay with Silu Granny.

Meanwhile, the boy from Hill Road had become obsessed after that one movie date. He kept calling and calling. She finally agreed to go for a drive with him.

He took her to Bandstand and parked his car. And while she was talking, he unzipped his pants and flashed his dick at her. OMG!

She was horrified. It was the first dick she had ever seen, and it looked scary—like a thin, red, throbbing one-eyed snake. She stopped meeting him.

But then Brinjal Boy wrote letters, buried them under her home and told her friend Sonia to ask her to dig them out and read them. He would wait for her to leave home and then follow her in his red Maruti.

She was scared and overwhelmed by his stalker behaviour. So, finally she decided to set things straight.

She agreed to meet him. They went for a drive on a wet monsoon afternoon in his Maruti along the sea at Bandstand.

She fidgeted. 'I don't like you. I don't want to be your girlfriend. That thing you flashed at me was disgusting. It looks like a snake. Please leave me alone.'

Silence reigned for three minutes. She was relieved. He had finally understood. He had got the picture.

The silence broke with the sound of a hard slap. It was her cheek. He stopped the car and glared at her, his face turning red. Humiliated, she jumped out of the car in the pouring rain. *How dare he!* She marched off, trying to look as elegant as she could as the Mumbai monsoon drenched her.

Brinjal Boy screamed after her, 'You little bitch, you think you're so cool because of Pink Panther? You think you are a big model now? Look what I got you.' He threw a bag out of the car. 'You don't need to model, I just bought you the clothes.'

She stopped and thought for a minute. She was tempted to look in the bag, but good sense prevailed over her sixteen-year-old self.

'I am no Julia Roberts, you are no Richard Gere. I don't need your charity. I will earn my Pink Panther clothes. Goodbye!' she yelled, walking away with dignity and drenched hair.

The sound of a car accelerating made her turn back around. Brinjal Boy was headed straight for her. Brinjal Boy from Hill Road had slapped her and was now trying to run her over! There was something surreal about this entire situation. This taught her something about men and their egos but there was no time to stop and take that lesson in.

He came after her at full speed. She was running in the middle of a heavy downpour on Bandstand, a red Maruti chasing her. She couldn't believe this was happening. She dodged stray cows, jumped over a stray dog but he was still in hot pursuit.

She tried to scream but nothing came out of her mouth. This felt like a bad dream. Her sandal flew off her foot to the other side of the road as she ran. But there was no way of retrieving it, she realized, as she turned back and found the bumper of his car in close proximity. She jumped off the parapet on to the rocks and ran, not turning back. She hid among the rocks with the smell of poo, her clothes sticky, her hair worse than the wet dog's that was licking her ankles.

An hour later, she slowly emerged from behind the rocks, took a rickshaw and fled home with one shoe, fully drenched.

She gave Granny a big hug as soon as she stepped in. She was soaking wet, her mascara smudged all over her face. Silu Granny looked at her suspiciously with one eye.

'Did you eat my cutlet?'

RECIPE:

Butter popcorn

LESSON LEARNT

1. Boys have egos the size of Mount Everest. Especially when it comes to their nether regions.

2. Just as the layers of tiramisu can be delicate and easily disrupted, so can a boy's ego.

WHERE IS HE NOW?

No idea.

She hopes she never sees Brinjal Boy and his one-eyed snake ever again.

5

Is Marrying Your First Love
a Terrible Idea?

Fear had her hiding at home. She was counting the days till the Pink Panther shoot. The night before, her phone lit up with a call from the photographer for the shoot.

'Hello?'

'Hey, I just called to inform you that you don't need to do the shoot, but don't worry, I'll make sure you still get the clothes from Pink Panther.'

'WHAT?! NO! NO!'

She was stunned. 'I'm going to do this shoot and earn the clothes,' she insisted.

She had fought with her family, forsaken the Goa vacation and had been almost run over by Brinjal Boy. She was *determined* to earn those clothes. The photographer sighed. *These crazy ideas agencies have, picking up kids.*

'Okay then, see you tomorrow.'

The next day a car pulled up at 5 a.m. outside Vina Villa, thanks to her tenacity. A tall, dark young man in

RayBan sunglasses got out. He didn't look old enough to be the photographer but he commanded respect among all the models in the car. Maybe it was his height; he was tall like the Burj Khalifa. The car was headed to Mukesh Mills.

It was a fun day where she got to try on many clothes and pose. The other models were tall, slim and much older. They snickered at her, and for a moment, she felt like she was back in school with Ameesha Sippy, but she held her head high and smiled for the camera.

Burj Khalifa was impressed. She had professionalism, was hard working and didn't complain when asked to change thirty-five times. He asked her to participate in a fashion show. They would pay her Rs 2000.

OMG Rs 2000! The obvious answer to this was 'Yes', and she began attending rehearsals unbeknown to her parents.

At that time, rehearsals were headed by a young Sarah Khan who was the choreographer of the show. Driven and fierce, Sarah Khan did not hesitate to reprimand the young model for being lost in her head and zoning out or forgetting her entries or for smiling. Smiling was a big NO in fashion shows because the models had to look edgy and unapproachable. And this was hard for her young, smiley impressionable self. She closed her mouth, intent on being professional.

A month later the show was ready. There was, however, one tiny detail that she had conveniently ignored. The show was in Goa and her parents didn't know. Thankfully, Burj Khalifa and an annoyed Sarah

Khan agreed to go the girl's house and ask her parents for permission.

They sat on the sofa in the living room between her parents as her father grilled them like a detective in an interrogation room.

'What is a fashion show? Why do people do fashion shows? Why do they walk up and down? Why is their expression so sad? What do you gain from this? Who is the audience?'

To her endless embarrassment, he asked what seemed to be a 100 more humiliating questions.

'Is this your profession? What is the profit margin? How much money do you spend on this fashion show? How much do you earn? What ambitions do you have from life? Is this a real job, this choreography? Do people actually buy clothes after watching children walk down the ramp? Why do you want my daughter? What does she have with fashion? Why Goa?'

He then turned to look at Sarah Khan.

'Will you be doing this kind of work for the rest of your life? What do your parents think?'

Sarah replied that she was thirty years old and her parents had passed away. Her father looked away, his slight embarrassment perhaps a tenth of what his daughter was feeling. However, he didn't let this deter him. At the end of the hour-long conversation, sorry, interrogation, he smiled and shook their hands, a clear sign of dismissal.

'I'm sorry. We had already decided before you came that she will not go to Goa with you for this fashion show. We have no interest in this fashion business but good luck on your show!'

She stared at him with utter disbelief. All those questions, all that humiliation, for nothing?

That night, she threw the biggest tantrum of her life. Her father was stubborn and told her he had made up his mind and there was no changing it. What he didn't know was that she too had made up her mind and there was *no* changing it.

The bus for Goa was leaving in three days and she *would* be on it. She packed a bag, wrote a note to her parents, wrapped a dupatta around her face, kissed Silu Granny on her head while she was sleeping. Then, she sneaked out of her home in the dead of night, took a rickshaw to Hill Road and climbed on to the Mumbai to Goa bus just as it started moving. She had run away from home.

On the bus she unwound the dupatta with a flourish. Her beaming face was the picture of victory, and her stunt had everyone on the bus clapping. She immediately spotted Burj Khalifa who had an empty seat waiting for her next to the window. She tried to control her burgeoning grin as she sashayed to the back of the bus, next to the young man. Soon, she noticed how weird he was acting. He kept fidgeting. His voice took her by surprise.

'You are a really lovely person,' he said.

'Thank you!' she replied.

'You didn't let us down.'

'I couldn't have.'

'I've grown very fond of you. You're a sweet, good, kind-hearted person from a er . . . lovely family.'

Lovely family? After the stunt her father pulled? This entire conversation is weird, she thought. *Weird, but nice.* She smiled again, looking out of the window.

'Not to mention beautiful. You are the most beautiful girl I've ever seen.'

Her head started to buzz with equal parts happiness and confusion.

'I think I am falling in love with you.'

Her head stopped buzzing. She was shocked. This was so unexpected that she could do nothing but gape at him. He charged on, looking at her.

'You don't have to feel the same way. I just wanted to let you know.'

She stared at him. And continued staring. The lack of expectations on his part was a novel concept for her. Struck speechless by his confession, she squeezed his hand in an effort to convey what she was feeling. Only, she herself couldn't identify any emotion in the mess that were her feelings, except gratitude.

He jumped up and yelled, 'She said YES!' Everyone clapped. She continued to be surprised and speechless.

And that was the beginning of her first real relationship. Even though it started off without her fully on board, she soon grew very fond of him. He was smart, funny, driven but mostly very kind, caring and mature; after all, he was six years older than her.

They travelled to Goa every few months. In the 1990s, Tito's was just a shack where they ate chocolate brownies.

They rented bikes and explored the town, went to their first rave together and had their own little shack on Candolim. Even though the shack didn't really belong to them, they still thought of it as their own and dreamt of how they would move there, catch fish for a living and swim in the quiet and clean Candolim sea for their entire lives. They couldn't even imagine Candolim would look like what it does today.

Once, as they were frolicking around in the ocean, he got bitten by a jelly fish. He yelped and ran out. She ran after him. With tears in his eyes and screaming, he fell in the hot sand . . . at the feet of two topless women with the largest breasts she had ever seen. There was nobody else on the quiet beach.

'Oh my God!' they screamed in their sexy French accents. 'Poor boy, he needs lime. Go get some lime,' they yelled at her while they checked out his jelly fish bite; their bare breasts all over him.

'Er, okay,' she said and ran in the blazing heat to the shack to get the lime. She ran back with it, the sun beating down on her. He was still in extreme pain and had tears in his eyes when she came back. 'Ice, we need ice for him,' said one of the topless French girls who was now cradling him in her arms.

She gulped pangs of jealousy as she saw his head in between the woman's naked breasts but obediently ran back in the sun to get him ice. When she went back, she saw he was smiling and talking to the girls in French. 'I didn't know you knew French,' she said, a little annoyed, as one of the girls rubbed his legs with ice while the other one massaged his head.

'I think he's okay now. Do you want to go?' she asked him. He looked at her face, excused himself and thanked the girls. 'Merci merci,' he said. She made a face. And they went back to the shack.

He laughed at her and hugged her as he saw her sweaty upset face.

'I have eyes only for you,' he said.

'But they had the biggest breasts I have ever seen.'

'So what?' he said, 'You're the one I love and desire.'

He kissed her. She felt a sense of relief. He was a good boyfriend. He never pressurized her to have sex with him even though he could easily have.

She helped him apply for his first big job at Lintas, an advertising agency, and he helped her navigate her modelling career, which had taken off quite nicely. She had a lot of respect for his advice and opinion. Six years was a big gap at that age. Plus, he was just generally very mature because he ran his entire home and was responsible for his five sisters and parents.

He had had a lot of sex and girlfriends before her. She had never had sex. But he didn't make her feel bad about wanting to wait.

He absolutely spoilt her. Not with luxuries or expensive gifts but with his heart. He was her best friend, her confidant, her sounding board, her mentor.

His father was unwell, so he had been working since he was seventeen. He was burdened with running the house but he never complained. He was always joking and laughing.

His house was modest, and his room was a little balcony that they had enclosed. All that fit was a single bed. His bed didn't cater to his long body. At six feet two inches, his feet would adorably stick out. They hung out in his room (balcony) with the door ajar, kissing for hours. When his mother or sister called, they would spring apart and pretend to read. His mom would bring rajma chawal in silver *thaalis*. Ravenous, they'd gobble it up and then kiss again until the next rajma chawal break.

One day, when her parents weren't home, she invited him to her home. They went to her parents' room and messed around.

Suddenly there was a loud knocking sound. They were interrupted by Silu Granny pounding on the door. She wanted to watch *The Bold and the Beautiful* and the living room TV had stopped working.

Granny's insistence and the lack of escape routes led to Granny sitting and watching TV on the edge of the bed, while the poor Burj Khalifa hid under the bed entirely naked with his toes sticking out. Granny watched two entire shows and then decided she wanted to take a nap on the bed, while the poor boy lay uncomfortably on the cold floor. Finally, when she heard Granny snoring, she ushered him out, threw his clothes at him and made him run out of the house.

He was a good boyfriend. What she didn't realize then was that he wasn't just a good boyfriend, he was a spectacular one. He would ruin other men for her. She didn't know this would happen; after all he was her first real boyfriend. He made her feel safe, but she didn't know what it was like to feel insecure. He made her feel beautiful, but she didn't know what it was like to be made to feel ugly. He made her feel cared for and looked after, but she didn't know what neglect felt like. She scribbled in her notes, 'Will marrying my first love feel like wearing oversized granny panties—familiar, comfortable and easy. But can I wear the granny panties my whole life?'

On her nineteenth birthday, he threw her a surprise party and invited all her friends. While cutting the cake, she felt her knife getting stuck on something. It was something solid that she was unable to cut through. Something was hidden under the chocolate.

'*Oh my God, please make it be a Discman.*'

With that hopeful thought, she plunged her hand into the chocolate and tried to pull out whatever there was underneath it, but it felt a lot smaller than a Discman.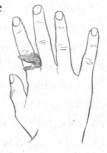

A small box. Her breath quickened and her heart raced.

Everyone screamed as she opened it, shaking. It was a RING! An alligator ring!

She had no idea why it was an alligator, but as everyone yelped with joy, she started sweating. Her pulse started beating fast. She started feeling very anxious. OH MY GOD! She wasn't ready to settle down. She wanted to see the world and she wanted to . . . she wanted to meet other men. (Oh my God, was she a bad person?) She *was not* ready to get tied up or tied down.

She knew her eyes had started wandering. She'd caught herself distracted by the hot Israeli boys in Goa and by the French guys and their accents and by the Spanish men who needed no commentary to justify their mention. Burj had seen her roving eye. He had tried to brush it off laughing, but he admitted it had made him uncomfortable when an Israeli guy had just picked her up and thrown her in the water in Goa as she giggled. She didn't want to look at other boys, but she was nineteen and she was curious, especially with foreigners.

She knew it would be wrong to accept the ring.

She politely asked if she could make it into a pendant and wear it around her neck. 'Of course,' he said.

But she could see the lump in his throat as he pretended to smile.

She was feeling commitment wary. How could she marry her first boyfriend? What about the *Sex and the City* life she imagined for herself?

So, when Tommy Chidambaram—a dark, half Indian, half American guy with dark skin and green eyes—waltzed in and asked her and her bare ring finger to join him for soup after a Channel V audition, she said yes. They were at Cafe Royal, a restaurant she had visited often with her boyfriend. She slurped mulligatawny soup and stared into Tommy's colourful eyes. His brown skin shone as he laughed at all her jokes and listened intently to her stories and ran his fingers up her thigh. She felt herself very attracted to Tommy Chidambaram. She felt so wrong, but it felt so exciting.

That night, she called Burj Khalifa from the landline.

As they spoke about how their day had been, she told him that she went to Cafe Royal. She could hear his breath on the other end of the line. He asked her if she went alone. She hesitated and then muttered a no. There was silence on the line, punctuated only by their rhythmic breathing.

'I went with Tommy Chidambaram.'

'You like him?' he asked.

'I think he's attractive, I'm sorry, I'm attracted to him,' she replied, feeling so awful.

He hung up and just like that they never spoke again. The relationship ended abruptly.

All because of mulligatawny soup.

As she lay in bed that night, she wondered, 'In relationships, is honesty truly the best policy?'

But then, this is what she had wanted. She had wanted freedom. She had not known how to ask for it.

'I hope there is nothing like relationship karma,' she told her friends.

They laughed, 'All is fair in love and break ups, wasn't that your line?' She nodded.

She went out with Tommy Chidambaram for a few more dates where his hand kept creeping up her skirt. But when one night she slapped his hand away and he didn't drop her home from Churchgate to Bandra, she stopped seeing him.

He wrote her poetry:

'I'm so sorry, my dear, for the cab ride you had
    to take,
Your upper lip glistens like honey, a sweet,
    sugary bake.
Beads of sweat between your brows, like pearls
    in a row,
I find it all so enchanting, that smile's adorable glow.
Your cute dimples on the corners, they make my
    heart sway,
I promise in the future, I'll taxi you all the way.'

She thought it to be personal, sweet and flattering.

But she missed Burj Khalifa, his stability, his *groundedness*. She didn't feel right with Tommy, he was charming and all, but Burj Khalifa was home.

'He is so kind, such a good guy,' she said as she cried to Gunjan and Sonia, her eighteen-year-old best friends. 'Oh, there are so many kind, good guys in the world,' the girls said naively.

She called Burj Khalifa several times. Again and again and again.

But he had let her go.

She needed to see the world and he knew it.

She never ate mulligatawny soup again.

RECIPE:

Rajma chawal

LESSON LEARNT

1. When you love someone set them free, sounds cliched but that's what Burj did for her.

2. Your first love is like eating khichdi, but over time, you might start to crave different flavours, explore new tastes and discover that there are other dishes out there that could tantalize your palate.

WHERE IS HE NOW?

Burj Khalifa is now a successful film-maker. He made a movie that was a huge hit. She was so proud when she saw his name in the credits that she cried! He's happily married and has two kids. He doesn't look her in the eye when he runs into her. She still remembers his phone number. It's a 98200 number. But she does not dial it. She just wishes the best for him always!

THREE THANK YOU'S AND A SORRY:

1. She thanks him for being her first real relationship and setting the bar high for all the men to follow.

2. She thanks him for being her mentor.

3. She thanks him for loving her purely, unselfishly with all his heart.

She is sorry she was unempathetic and didn't end the relationship with compassion and love.

SHE MISSES:

1. His advice.

2. His care.

3. How he found everything she said amusing.

6

Once the Unattainable becomes Attainable, does Love End?

It was now time for her to see the world. To see the world *and* the biggest lust of her life so far—the Dirty Dancing Dude, the charismatic musician she'd fallen for in college and the reason why the number on the size tag of her clothes had reduced. He would often show up in her dreams, serenading her.

'Baby, my sweet baby, you're the one tan tara tan tan tan tara.'

Clearly *Dirty Dancing* had been quite a psychological experience for her. She'd think about how he looked a lot like Patrick Swayze—his sharp jawline, long hair and his pouty lips. She imagined him lifting her up in the pool like Patrick Swayze did with Jennifer Gray.

All this dreaming only made her more determined. She obsessively checked the balance of her bank account. Every day she would pray for the numbers to reach Rs 35,000—that was how much she needed to buy a ticket to New York City. No more Fashion Street—she gave up shopping to save for the ticket. Every penny counted!

A year later, all that dreaming and all that saving paid off. She finally had Rs 35,000. She was finally on her way to Dirty Dancing Dude and the *coolest* city in the world.

She bit her nails as she emailed him. This was the bravest thing she had ever done.

Dear Dirty Dancing Dude, this is Buffalo Butt. Do you remember me from Xavier's? I will be in New York this summer. Would you like to meet me?

To her surprise and joy, he replied immediately.

Of course, I remember you. Come, I will show you around the best city in the world, Ms Buffalo-with-a-cute-face.

Cute face! She was shaking with excitement, counting the days and her savings.

Her parents had no idea who Dirty Dancing Dude was. All they needed to know was that she was going to stay with a college friend.

Silu Granny, though, would smile at her funny when she mentioned America and even though Granny, too, didn't know about Dirty Dancing Dude, these smiles made her suspicious of her knowledge on the topic.

She was graduating from Xavier's that year. If things went according to plan, she was to leave two days after her final exams. She had bought her ticket, for Rs 35,000, on Air India, six months ago. She had another Rs 20,000 saved for her travel. She didn't go out to eat with her friends, she didn't spend on anything. She was going to go to America and sleep on Dirty's couch!

Plans though, no matter how meticulously devised, rarely turn out the way expected. She learnt this when her pale-faced, worried father shattered her game plan and a little bit of her heart, a day after her last exam, with a few words.

'I don't think you should go to America.'

'What, no, why, what do you mean, Dad? The flight is tomorrow. I saved for the ticket, it's non-refundable, so why are you being so *cruel*? I've even left the phone number and address with you. It's my college friend. Why are you . . .'

She geared up for a fight. But his soft words stopped any further protests.

'Honey . . . Silu Granny has cancer. I won't tell you to do anything. This is your decision to make. You can go but there is no guarantee about Granny's heath. It's your choice.'

With those words, he walked away, leaving a confused and heartbroken nineteen-year-old, standing alone in her room, knowing she won't get any sleep that night.

The next day she found herself sitting on a plane to New York, between two large, hairy men. Granny would be fine, she was a fighter. *Granny had to be fine.* She wasn't going to accept anything else. This blind conviction in Silu Granny's recovery allowed the solemn granddaughter to let a tiny bit of excitement seep in.

I am finally going to New York!

New York, for its part, lived up to its reputation. *It truly is the coolest city*, she thought as she looked around in awe. It was buzzing with electricity, pulsating with energy, vibrant with young people from all over the world; she felt as if she had found home. But she didn't allow herself to lose focus. She was there to meet Dirty Dancing Dude.

They had decided to meet outside Mc Donald's on Times Square. She was wearing skinny black pants

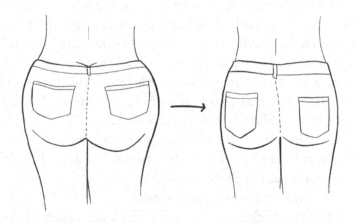

It was a carefully made choice that would make him notice her smaller figure. And notice he did. His first comment was that the buffalo had turned into a swan!

She smiled, *this is exactly what I had imagined*. He invited her to dinner. They went to some ethnic restaurant in Queens. She was so nervous. Her hands were shaking.

They ordered a kale and feta pizza. As she tried to cut her pizza, she felt her hands shake. She was so nervous around him. Her stomach churning with butterflies and her hands trembling. She kept trying to cut the pizza with her fork and knife but her shaky hands were not cooperating with her idea of being eloquent. 'Your hands are shaking, Buffalo Butt,' he said, pointing out the obvious. She bit her lip embarrassed, and her hand slipped and the pizza flew across the room. There was a big pause. Time stopped. Everyone turned. The gorgeous kale and feta pizza was sitting on the floor. She went red.

Dirty got up, walked towards it and smoothly picked it up. He gracefully walked back to the table. She watched him in slo-mo. He looked like a prince carrying her fallen pizza. He laughed casually. 'You're really cute,' he said. She blushed. He picked up a piece of the pizza with his hand and shoved it in his mouth. She smiled and did the same. She was thankful to him for making her feel comfortable. She felt less nervous now.

Afterwards, they walked to his apartment.

He told her he roomed with two other guys, but she could have his couch for the night.

She was so happy to be his guest.

But that night, she got a call from her father as she was trying to transform the couch into a makeshift bed. The entire episode is fuzzy in her head, her memory shadowed by his words.

'Granny is no more. She's gone. She was suffering and in pain so this may be better for her. The funeral is tomorrow. You won't make it even if you get on a flight now. So don't bother, just stay there and complete your trip.'

She threw up violently in the bathroom. All that fancy pizza wasn't feeling so fancy in her belly anymore.

She couldn't sleep at all. Silu Granny's face kept showing up, smiling and patting her head.

The next morning she woke up with puffy eyes and an aching chest. She sat up and noticed Dirty staring at her from across the room while tying his shoelaces. His eyes shone with tenderness.

This was the look she had been dreaming about. This was the moment she had imagined. 'I'm glad you came here Buffalo Butt, you're a cutie.'

But there were no butterflies, there was no tenderness in her. In the morning light, his jaw looked too protruding, his hair too oily, his lips too dry.

'I have to go home,' she said. 'My grandmother left us last night.'

He sat next to her and helped her book her flight. Everything was a daze after that.

Back home, she struggled to find familiarity. She would go to the kitchen and open the fridge—there were no cutlets with notes on them. She would go to the bathroom—there were no buckets filled with water. The house felt empty—there were no old lady shoes shifting around the house. Her mother told her that she could move into Granny's room. She would finally have her own room, one she wouldn't share with her sister.

The next day she woke up in Granny's bed. She sat up, looked down at her legs. Strong, thick, muscular legs.

A voice inside her said, 'I have Silu Granny legs.'

A crow sat on the window. She took a deep breath. A tear ran down her face.

Recipe

Feta and kale pizza

Lesson Learnt

1. No boy can replace GRANNY!

2. There's a difference between love and infatuation.

3. Infatuation is like an exhilarating roller-coaster ride, with the highs and lows but it also stops abruptly as soon as the ride ends.

4. Infatuation can be as bewildering as trying to eat spaghetti with a spoon—it leaves you feeling like a bit of a mess.

Where Is He Now?

Dirty Dancing Dude now lives in Miami with his blonde wife and four kids. He has a travel agency. They are friends on Facebook.

7

Do No Butterflies Mean No Love?

She walked in with bags full of clothes, dumped them on her desk and sighed loudly. The MTV office in Mumbai was a messy, crowded space with lots of desks in one small room. It was usually filled with young people, some playing Solitaire, others on Facebook.

Suddenly, a tall, skinny guy with a mop of curly hair burst into the room, sprinting past her and down the hall.

Realizing he was going the wrong way, he turned and raced back in a flurry. The look on his face screamed that he wasn't well. His hand covered his mouth, his eyes looking around anxiously.

'Men's room?' the tall, skinny guy asked frantically.

She paused to think for a second. 'Um . . . um, I think the closest . . .'

But it was too late. The tall guy grabbed a trash bin, shoved his head in it and retched, leaving the young women in the office shrieking in horror. When he was done, he wiped his mouth with a handkerchief, then turned back to her.

'Sorry, that was sort of a surprise. I just . . .'

Suddenly, his face went white. Oh, there was more. He leapt for the trash bin again. And HEAVED.

Co-worker (on phone), 'I have no idea what that sound is, Mr Mehta. Must be a bad connection.'

After round two, the tall skinny guy's face had turned bright red. His eyes were watery and bloodshot, and the whole office was staring.

'Are you all right?' she asked tentatively.

'I don't think so.' He held up a finger, 'Just a minute . . .', like he was waiting for something and said, 'Okay. Yeah. Now I am.'

'What did you eat?' she asked.

He smiled bashfully and said, 'If you ever see that guy selling mutton curry off a cart pulled by a . . . (can't remember exactly) I dunno . . . by a mutton, maybe? Delicious. Highly recommended.'

Some office girls giggled. He was cute in a nerdy sort of way.

'I gotta say, it was worth it,' he declared to the whole office and then he coughed and his eyes went wide and teary again. She ventured to ask him if he needed a doctor or anything.

To which he said, 'Oh, this is nothing. I was in China a month ago. Both ends.'

She found herself making a face at that.

'I'm the new promo guy,' the tall, skinny promo guy continued and extended his hand. She looked down at it uncomfortably, imagining where it had been and made a namaste instead. 'I'm the stylist here but I'm leaving soon. Going to Singapore,' she said.

'What's in Singapore?' the promo guy asked. There were a lot of things but she had her future tacked on Singapore Airlines. She had been offered a job and when she told him this, it was his turn to make a face.

'Hey, it's not so bad. I will travel the world and save money and then go to New York and learn film-making.'

'You're not from here?' she asked.

'I'm from New York, actually,' he replied. 'I'm an ABCD.'

'Huh?' She was confused.

He continued, 'American Born Confused Desi, fresh off the boat, straight into this glorious wholesome country. Small detour in China but nothing prepares you for

India. The motherland. The mother's land and father's, but they are both in America now and I'm here. They

are separated. Divorced actually. They hate each other. I always wonder how two people who can love each other, enough to elope and run away to another country, can end up hating each other so much.'

She nodded. *That's a lot of personal details for our first conversation.*

'Mom was a Brahmin from south India. Dad, a Muslim from Mohammed Ali Road. Mom put sleeping powder in her dad's milk, ran away and got married to my dad. They moved to America and had three kids. Now, they HATE each other. Oh, I've made a movie on it. Would you like to watch it?'

Awkward and unsure of what to say, she asked, 'Er . . . I . . . are you the guy who made the Liftboy promo?'

'Ya, that's me,' he replied.

'And the idli dosa promo?'

'Guilty.'

'Wow! You're really talented,' she said excitedly.

'So that's a yes?' he continued mischievously.

He fell on the floor holding his heart. She found herself laughing.

Promo Guy then went on to establish his musicality. 'India is my motherland. The food's great and the girls are pretty,' he sang with a wink. She had never met anyone so exuberant and upbeat. Just as she was thinking this, she heard a loud voice from the adjacent office. It was Mr Lulla, the MTV boss.

'Could you come to my office, Miss?'

Abruptly, without missing a beat, she said to Promo Guy, 'Do not eat from the roads. It's not for you NRI ABCD types.' And then, she ran into Mr Lulla's office.

'I hear you are leaving MTV to join Singapore Airlines?'

She nodded.

Mr Lulla had a quizzical expression on his face. 'I don't understand. We offered you a job to be a veejay but you said you wanted to be in production.'

'Yes and then Namrata Malhotra said I had no experience in production so she made me a stylist,' she clarified.

Mr Lulla wasn't having any of it. 'And now you are going to be an air hostess?'

'I want to see the world, Sir,' she interjected.

'You have a natural talent. We can tell. Take the veejay job.'

She shook her head. 'I want to live in Singapore.'

'We will base you in Singapore. That's where our head office is.'

She stared at him.

'Either you see the world or the world sees you. I advise you to think about this very carefully.' He promptly went back to his paperwork without another glance. His yellow and red socks smiled at her from under the table.

The next day she called Singapore Airlines and told them she had stubbed her toe and couldn't take the job. Yes, great excuse.

A month later, she was in Singapore, in a cute little apartment, ready to start her new job with MTV as a veejay.

That afternoon, the door bell rang. She shuffled towards the door and opened it. And, what do you know?

Promo Guy was standing there with a bunch of flowers in his arms.

'What are you doing here?' she asked.

'They transferred me here too. Now, do you want to watch the movie I made?'

She gave him a hug, elated to see him.

And there it was, the start of a beautiful FRIENDSHIP.

Promo Guy taught her how to use email. She had never used the Internet before. He set up a Hotmail account for her. She had never lived alone before. He taught her how to clean her apartment. He made her lift the chairs and get the *goochis* (that  was what he called the balls of hair and dust that you find when cleaning) as he sang songs and made jokes.

They woke up every morning and danced to Eros Ramozotti. They'd sing while he cooked breakfast, and then run around the city shooting videos. He taught her a few more tricks. Most importantly, he taught her about cameras. It was fun. They had so many similar interests.

They travelled to Bali for a long weekend. They ran up and down the paddy fields like in *DDLJ*, singing and dancing. She had never met anyone so smart and so fun.

But somehow that was all the chemistry they had. A great friendship chemistry. He talked to her about his redheaded ex-girlfriend, with whom he used to have sex in the middle of the night. He talked a lot about his sexual escapades with other women. She told him about Burj Khalifa.

She wasn't feeling that romantic chemistry. There were no butterflies. But they were so close. Like a couple.

One evening, they were cooking mutton curry together. And he bent in and kissed her. She kissed him back.

It felt awkward. She felt like she was kissing her friend. That night after a lot of wine, they went ahead and kissed again. It felt so weird.

Later, when he was asleep, she went to her balcony that overlooked Orchard Street and cried. She missed Burj Khalifa and the way she felt when she was with him.

They never tried to kiss again. But they continued to be in a situationship. He was her only companion in Singapore.

But Promo Guy had to go back to New York eventually.

He drew a map for her on how she could eventually get to New York and work for MTV there. She hugged him good bye, sad he was leaving. They both knew the friendship was something that they would always treasure.

Recipe

Mutton curry

LESSON LEARNT

1. Friends without benefits can be the better choice, in some cases.

2. Sometimes there will be no butterflies and you can't force it.

3. Love does not have to be physical attraction—it can be a shared sense of humour, getting each other's quirks that don't necessarily lead to romantic sparks.

4. Not having butterflies is like trying to fly without wings or a cup of tea without a biscuit.

Where is he now?

Promo Guy is one of the most successful ad film-makers in the world now.

They are not in touch.

His Russian girlfriend, who is also his assistant, checks his email accounts and does not want him to be in touch with any women.

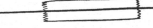

Three thank you's and a sorry:

1. She thanks him for teaching her how to use the computer.

2. She thanks him for being her first film school.

3. She thanks him for being her first window into the Western world.

She is sorry there were no butterflies.

SHE MISSES:

1. His interesting stories.

2. Learning all aspects of film-
    making from him.

3. Just being his friend.

8

SHOULD EVERY GIRL DATE A FRENCHMAN AT LEAST ONCE IN HER LIFE?

Singapore was lonely after Promo Guy left. Besides her work colleagues, who were not very friendly and who disappeared after 5 p.m., she knew nobody there.

She spent her weeknights and weekends watching movies in the theatre alone, chomping on sushi rolls. Weekends were spent by the pool in her apartment. It was a great lifestyle but her only friend was loneliness.

As for boyfriends, most Chinese men did not even seem to notice her while the white men in Asia seemed interested only in Asian women. Not Indian kind of Asian but South-East Asian.

She was very, very single and friendless.

So, one night, she googled 'Indian Party in Singapore', and after finding one she thought was worth trying, she mustered the courage to go alone. She circled around the party three times.

Once in, she went straight to the bar counter. *A couple of drinks will help loosen me up.* She awkwardly stood there by the bar smiling at random people. Most didn't smile back. An hour and three Smirnoff Ice's later, out of the crowd appeared a tall hip looking Indian girl who walked straight up to her.

'Hi I'm Malini. Cool dress.'

'Nice top,' she complimented back.

Just then, a cute Indian boy passed by them. They both turned to look.

'Cute smile,' she said checking the boy out.

'Sexy butt,' Malini joined in. They broke into a fit of giggles.

And that's how she made her first friend in Singapore.

Malini was the queen of Singapore's expat community. She worked in a bank and in the evenings they partied together. Malini could outdrink any man. She was confident, smart and she knew everyone.

Through Malini, she met the entire Indian community and some cute expat boys.

Malini even set up her first date in Singapore with Le French Homme (the Frenchman).

He was thinner than the type she usually liked, but he was sweet, attentive and very complimentary.

He crossed and uncrossed his legs like Sharon Stone when he sat, sipping on a girly cocktail. This was very unlike most boys she knew from back home. He would get up and kiss her on both cheeks when she'd arrive. He was into her, she felt it. And she liked the attention. He had a sophistication that wasn't flashy and was not afraid to wear pink.

She learnt quickly that Frenchmen didn't feel the need to prove their masculinity. They were comfortable with their feminine side.

'You're like Bridget Bardot. You're both cute and sexy. It's very difficult to decide which one . . .' he said with his French accent in full effect.

She giggled.

'You're my Esmeralda. My little gypsy. Let me cook you dinner, my Esmeralda Gypsy Bardot.'

And so the romance started. She went over to his house for dinner. He lived with Hughes, his roommate, whom she found more attractive. Le French Homme set the table like they were in a restaurant. He lit candles, played Manu Chao, arranged flowers and asked her to pick from ten wines and then served her an aperitif—an alcoholic drink served before a meal to stimulate the appetite.

On the menu was French onion soup topped with melted, toasted cheese.

She dug past the cheese, trying to get to the broth.

They both looked at her in shock.

'French onion soup with no cheese is not very good manners, my Bardot Esmeralda . . .' said Le French Homme.

'Oh . . .' she mumbled. 'But I can't eat too much cheese,' she exclaimed. 'It makes me fat and you won't like me then, will you?'

'Oh a little more flesh, I don't mind,' he exclaimed. 'Cheese is French . . .' said Hughes.

'It's just French! Eat it, don't worry, we like you a little plump.'

She laughed and slurped up the cheese.

Next they brought out huge loaves of bread and a small piece of fish. She scarfed down the fish in one bite.

'Oh, I was just about to pour the wine that went with the fish,' Le French Homme said.

She stared at him wide eyed.

'Oops, I finished it.'

'Before I even served the wine . . .'

'It's great. Can I er . . . have some more?'

They laughed.

'My little gypsy has an appetite,' he exclaimed.

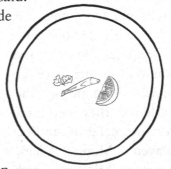

'The meal is over but "crème brûlée"?' he asked.

She nodded hungrily. She learnt quickly that French may eat baguettes and cheese but their portions were as big as her little finger . . . and every time she ate with them she had to go home and eat some more.

'It's just French! Sacré Français!' they exclaimed. That's how all the French women keep their petite figures.

And soon, this was her life in Singapore. She went to their place after work, all three of them drank a lot of wine together, and then they would bring out tiny portions of food after which she would insist on going home. Mostly because she wanted to eat the daal and rice that she made in her pressure cooker. One day, she was at their home. 'We need to get some more wine,' she exclaimed. 'Let me go change,' he said. 'You can just go like this,' she announced.

'To the grocery store in pyjamas?' They both turned to her shocked, that's not French.

'Oh!' she said.

They suggested a trip to Bali. She agreed.

The three of them flew to Bali, a short flight from Singapore. She sat in the middle, excited.

The first day, they took her to a black sand beach. It was beautiful. Sparkling black sand. She smiled, taking it all in. They opened some wine, ate some bread and cheese. This was fun, she thought.

But then, out of the blue, they both started throwing their clothes off. She stood there in shock, staring at the thin Frenchmen butt naked, their bottoms looking very white in the black sand.

'We French like to be nude on beaches,' explained Le French Homme.

'Oh,' she mumbled.

'Join us?'

'Er, no thank you. In my country we wear saris on the beach.'

The joke went over their heads.

'Okay, your wish . . .' they said.

And then they both started running naked on that black sand beach, laughing and singing French songs.

'It's just French! Sacré Français!'

The next day she got in her swimsuit and met them at the pool.

'Shouldn't we shower before we jump in?' she said.

'This is the bath,' said Le French Homme.

'Ew,' she exclaimed.

'I don't understand why you must shower all the time,' he said. 'Isn't that why perfume was invented?'

He pushed her in the water, laughing.

She opened her bag, pulled out a long thick baguette and chomped on it as she sat watching the nude Frenchmen frolic around.

'You should wear a swimsuit that covers half your bottom,' suggested Le French Homme.

'That would suit you very much,' Hughes chipped in. 'This one covers too much,' they both nodded in agreement.

'Oh, you should wear shoes with small heels.'

'But we are at the beach,' she exclaimed.

'And a yellow sarong would go with that,' Huges chimed in.

She soon learnt that it was normal for Frenchmen to critique outfits and offer advice on them. They meant no harm by it.

'It's just French! Sacré Français!'

They rented a van and drove around Bali, but these two men got lost all the time. And behind the wheel, their tempers flared, both of them yelling in French, '*Putain, Merde, Batard*,' at anyone who crossed the car. At night, when she asked them about it as they drank their wine, they said, 'We meant no harm by it. It's just French! Sacré Français!'

The two Frenchmen and she were in the hotel restaurant having a serious conversation about politics that turned dark and existential very quickly.

'Can we lighten the mood?' she said.

'We French are ready for both sex and death,' said Le French Homme. 'After all, we invented lingerie and the guillotine.'

'And French fries,' she said trying to be cute.

'And the French kiss,' said Le French Homme pulling her close. Hmm, he definitely knew how to kiss! The two men complained about the food.

'Should we send it back?' she asked. 'I like my dish but if you don't like it, order something else.'

'Oh we are enjoying it.'

'But you just complained that it had no taste,' she said.

The boys laughed. 'Complaining is part of the French culture, little gypsy, the food is fine. It's just French! Sacré Français!'

'Are Frenchmen better lovers?' her friends asked.

'Well, they definitely want to please you,' she replied. 'I could say more but that would not be French. The French don't kiss and tell,' she said and laughed.

In spite of all the great kissing, she decided she wasn't feeling this whole French thing, so when they returned to Singapore, she broke up with Le French Homme.

'We are just very different,' she told him.

Tears poured out of his blue eyes.

'I am heartbroken, my Bridget.'

'Well, firstly my name is not Bridget or Esmeralda,' she said. 'You never even say my real name,' she exclaimed. 'And I am not a gypsy.'

'I do not work for bank Paribas. I am a secret service agent, I work for the CIA,' said Le French Homme.

'Er, okay. I still don't feel that I am in love and shouldn't we be in love?' she said.

'I want to tell you all about my double life,' he said.

She couldn't tell if he was serious or joking.

'That's not going to change my mind,' she said.

He cried some more.

Le French Homme came over to her home every morning after that with a different thoughtful gift. One day it was a perfume, next day lingerie. 'We French do not wait for Valentine's Day to give gifts,' he announced.

'I am not changing my mind,' she said. He'd push past her, go to her kitchen and wash her dishes. Then he would take her hand in his and gently kiss the top of it. After this he would go to his job (at bank Paribas not the CIA).

It was all very French . . . Sacré Français.

It was her birthday; she was having a party at home. She now had some Indian friends, through Malini. They were very amused with the blue-eyed skinny Frenchman. They realized that every time they dropped something on the floor, he came running with a cloth and went on his knees and started cleaning. Soon they started doing this as a joke and saying, '*Dekho dekho pocha leke aa gaye.*'

She felt bad for the poor guy.

After the party, she spoke to Malini about this.

'He seems so heartbroken; I do not know what to do. Maybe I should give this a chance.'

Malini sipped on her whiskey and laughed.

'He and Hughes have been sleeping with my colleague Min this whole time. She can't stop bragging about her ménage à trois (threesome) with both of them.'

She sat there shocked. 'What? Why didn't you tell me before?'

'I don't know,' said Malini. 'You weren't even into him.'

'Ménage à trois? Threesome?'

Malini laughed. 'It's just French! Sacré Français!'

Recipe

French onion soup

LESSON LEARNT

1. Dating a Frenchman is an experience. They can make you feel appreciated and desirable like nobody else.

2. Men need NOT be macho to be masculine like the Frenchmen who embrace their masculine and feminine side.

3. They have the 'je ne se quoi' with their baguettes and their well-tailored clothes.

4. Dating a Frenchman is like eating a chocolate croissant, delicious but not a breakfast you can eat every day.

and

5. Hmm, eat small portions to have a petite figure.

WHERE IS HE NOW?

Le French Homme still works for Paribas. Still lives with Hughes. They have a cute little home in London and have adopted a baby. Sometimes they call her on Skype and sing her French songs. Sacré Français!

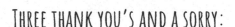

Three thank you's and a sorry:

1. She thanks him for teaching her the French language and culture, and showering her with French lingerie and perfume.

2 She thanks him for introducing her to Manu Chao.

3. She thanks him for making Singapore memorable for her.

She is sorry she made fun of him to her friends.

She misses:

1. Feeling like an exotic gypsy.

2. Hanging out and singing with the two crazy Frenchmen.

3. All the attention!

9
WHAT'S IT LIKE WITH A BRAZILIAN?

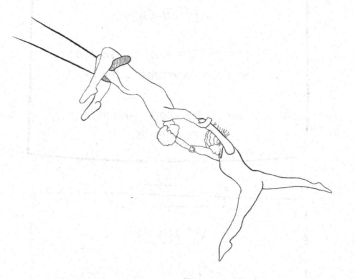

She was still in Singapore, suffering from a very dry patch. Chinese boys still looked through her. Expat boys only cared about Chinese girls.

Cirque Du Soleil was in town. For those who have never heard of the Cirque, it was a circus with a parade of wow moments filled with acrobatic wonders from around the world, who could freakishly walk on water with their arms. These circus people made quite a few appearances around town; they were all very fit and striking looking.

Among them, one in particular caught her eye. He was tall, dark and beautiful with big arms and a six-pack. He was the most beautiful man she had seen with a mane of thick, brown hair. She nicknamed him 'Six-pack'. Every time she saw Six-pack, her hormones danced a little happy dance.

Once, late at night, she was at Starbucks outside California Fitness Gym. The original plan was to work out but she had no motivation. She wasn't feeling too well and could feel a cold coming. Her belly felt as big and bloated as a watermelon. She didn't even have the will to wax her legs, and she was officially growing a moustache.

She missed home, missed family, missed friends, missed India and missed those hot Punjabi boys.

Work was good here in Singapore but . . .

Atishoooo!

Okay now I do have a cold. Ugh.

She sat there biting into her second bagel of the night. Bagels had been her latest discovery. Not knowing that bread was the enemy back then, she skipped dinner and gym every night and sat at Starbucks and ate bagels. *How many calories can pieces of bread with a hole in them have anyway?*

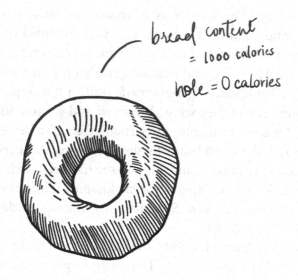

In the middle of her inner monologue, someone came and sat at the table next to her. She sneezed. It was one of those unexpected sneezes, you know the ones that just happen when you do not happen to have any tissue. She started to frantically look around for a tissue as her nose dripped. As she turned around, she noticed Six-pack sitting at the table next to hers.

Horrified, she rushed to the bathroom, blew her nose and wished she had some eyeliner. Her hair was doing something funny. She dabbed some water on it and then peered into her bag for some kind of make-up—*mascara? No. Eyeliner? No.* She sighed.

Not to forget, she was sporting a moustache. She walked out of the bathroom after a long time to get back to her bagel that she had lost appetite for to see that Six-pack was gone.

Oh well. Probably not the best time for her to make eyes at him. She picked the bagel up and as she bit into it, she felt a tap on her shoulder. She turned.

It was Six-pack. *Oh My God.* Her bagel fell.

'Oh oh sorry . . .' he said with a strong accent.

She was floored, as was her bagel. 'It's okay. I don't want it anyway.'

He responded with something in a foreign language.

'I don't understand what you're saying.'

'Posso me sentar,' he continued. *What is he saying? The accent was too strong. Wait! Was that English? Or Portuguese?*

'Huh?'

He pointed to the chair. Finally, understanding what he meant, she said 'Ya, sure.'

'My English no good . . .' he said as they sat down. 'Me Brazil. You know Brazil?'

'I have heard of it, yes.'

'I'm trying to practise my English.'

'Oh, I speak English, you can practise on me.' She started laughing nervously. *Gosh, that was too flirtatious and suggestive for her first sentence.*

She felt another sneeze coming. She thanked God for the toilet roll she'd taken from the bathroom. Just as she did, she stopped to think. *I can't take a toilet roll out from my bag in front of him . . . I . . . I . . .* ATISHOOOOOOOO!

He leapt up to get her some tissue as she tried to not let the snort drip out.

'Você tem um resfriado.' She stared at him blankly. He sneezed a fake sneeze and she laughed.

'In Brazil we can cure,' he said with a sexy grin.

'Rest? Sleep? Vitamin C?'

'Dance,' Six-pack replied confidently. She wasn't sure she was understanding him.

'Really? You dance your cold off in Brazil?'

But he answered her question with another one. 'Zouk. You come?'

'Er, you want me to go to the nightclub Zouk with you now?' she looked down and said with uncertainty.

'Yes' was his crisp answer. But, she pointed to her workout clothes. He shrugged.

Twenty minutes later, she found herself in Zouk in her trackpants dancing with Six-pack. She threw her backpack on the side and did her best to keep up with him. Note that this was a man from the circus whom she had seen on a trapeze with very few clothes on, walking on one hand on a rope and then somersaulting in the air and landing on a plank, just to moonwalk and then jump into a pool of water. How was she going to impress this man with her bhangra type dance moves?

He brought her a caipirinha, which she later found out was Brazil's national cocktail. She sipped on it. They held eye contact and danced. He wasn't trying to show off his dance steps and she appreciated that. He carried her once or twice on his shoulders. She laughed, every little cell of her on fire. Her heart was racing and her palms were sweating. She was drawn to him like bee to honey. She felt exhilarated, dizzy and happy. Maybe she had just been love sick. Her cold magically

disappeared after a glass of caipirinha. He whispered in her ear but she couldn't understand a word, so she just nodded.

Next, they moved to a party at the Pan Pacific Hotel on what seemed like the thirty-first floor. She wished she was not in her workout clothes as sexy girls in heels strutted by.

But he kept talking to her and she kept nodding. Both not understanding the other. As they walked on the terrace, he said something and she smiled. The smile must have been a giveaway because he then leaned in and kissed her. Right then, she thought she saw stars.

So *this is what they talk about in the movies and books.* He firmly held her hand and led her out of the room, into an elevator and into another room. His grip on her hand felt so strong and sexy. Soon, they entered a room and it was just him and her and a lot of mirrors.

Was she going to actually do this?

He kissed her again. *Oh yes, she was going to do this.*

He started pulling her legs towards him.

'Let alone a Brazilian, I haven't even waxed my legs,' she breathed out anxiously. But of course, he didn't understand.

'You want to stop?' he asked. She hesitated but felt every cell in her body screaming *HELL NO.*

The two of them were up all night, giggling. They finally fell asleep in each other's arms when the sun came up. She woke up with the sun in her eyes. He was up already, dressed to leave the room.

'You sleep. I come back.'

'Where are you going?'

'English lessons,' he said. 'And then I bring you.' He made a gesture for food. She looked at the gorgeous man and continued to smile.

'Thank you.'

He left with a final blinding smile aimed at her. She half fell asleep again and when she woke up, she gathered her things and left. She walked out of the hotel with a little pep in her step, feeling deliciously good.

She knew she couldn't have a relationship with Six-pack. They could barely communicate. It was what it was. A beautiful liberating experience that made her feel more like a woman than a girl. *Thank you, Six-pack!*

But this is not the end of the story with Six-pack. They kept in touch, having many wonderful times.

It was all beautiful and romantic in the beginning, but it all came crashing down one day when he got very upset when she went for dinner with her Singaporean boss, a short Chinese guy in whom she had no interest.

Six-pack confronted her in the restaurant and started yelling in Portuguese. She was embarrassed in front of her boss. That night he drank like crazy and then stormed out of the hotel room where he was staying, leaving her there. She had no way of even explaining herself to him.

They didn't meet for a few weeks but then got back together just a few days before the circus was leaving Singapore.

He tried to talk her into a long-distance relationship. However, they soon realized that while the language gap was tolerable in person, on the phone, it was practically impossible.

He asked her to leave her life and join the circus with him and travel the world being a circus-star's wife. She thought about it but couldn't begin to imagine how she'd break the news to her Indian parents.

Mom Dad, I am going to join the circus. That was not going to fly with any Indian family.

She declined.

RECIPE

Caipirinha, Brazil's national cocktail

LESSON LEARNT

1. Dating a Brazilian man is like doing the samba (their dance)—full of energy, passionate and quite complicated.

2. Being with a Brazilian is like sipping the caipirinha cocktail, intoxicating and refreshing at the same time.

3. Pros of dating a Brazilian guy
Very passionate
Great dancers
Lots of fun
Romantic

4. Cons of dating a Brazilian guy
Jealous and possessive
Moody

WHERE IS HE NOW?

Six-pack still has a six-pack, still works for the circus. They are friends on Facebook. The only difference is he has lost his hair.

He has a sexy wife with blonde dreadlocks who's covered in tattoos. She walks on water and does handstands on ropes.

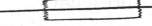

THREE THANK YOU'S AND A SORRY:

1. She thanks him for one of the most memorable nights of her life.

2. She thanks him for being the hottest guy she has ever seen.

3. She thanks him for inviting her to join the circus and travel the world with him.

She is sorry she couldn't accept his proposal to join the circus.

She misses:

1. His six-pack.

2. His Brazilian accent.

3. Watching him walk on his hands while holding a ball between his feet.

10

WHEN DID BEING SINGLE BECOME EQUIVALENT TO BEING DESPERATE?

She was back in India.

It was a lazy Sunday, and she was lounging around her parents' house when she got a call from Aunt Perizad, her father's youngest sister. Aunt Perizad was known as the meddler in the family. Warily, she answered the call.

'Hello?'

'You have to come over now!'

'Is it important? I'm kind of in the middle of something,'

'No NOW! There is a surprise waiting here for you. You will thank me.'

With no other choice, she heaved herself off the couch and prepared herself for the short trek to Aunty Perizad's house. She couldn't deny her curiosity, but you know what they say about curious cats.

At Aunt Perizad's home, there was a party on in full force. She cautiously entered the crowded room. It didn't escape her notice that all the aunties were staring at her and whispering. She hesitated.

I want to turn around and run. This is definitely a trap.

Despite that thought she kept walking. The whispering crowd slowly parted to make a path for her. A path that led her to a tall and fattish man, standing with his back to her.

At that moment, Aunt Perizad appeared out of nowhere and pushed her towards him. Unprepared, she lost her balance and bumped into him, almost knocking his glass out of his hand.

He turned around to investigate, and she immediately and uncomfortably begun to apologize.

'Oops. So sorry about that. I uh . . .' She turned to glare at her aunt but was momentarily distracted by his face. *It's a cute face.*

She fidgeted. 'Er . . . hello.'

He extended his hand. 'I'm Anal. Anal spelled ANAL,' he said smiling.

Her eyes widened. ANAL. *How could he say that with a straight face?*

With that thought, she shook his hand, which was wet. She smiled at him as she discreetly wiped her hand on her dress, slightly grossed out. Another aunty made a sudden appearance.

'Anal beta, I'd like to introduce you to her. She can cook Mediterranean and Italian food and is also an excellent swimmer. She has a driving and a diving license, and she goes to the gym every day because her figure is very important to her.'

'I er, I don't er . . .' she tried to get a word in, but her aunt kept going.

'And haan, she has a very nice wardrobe . . .' Auntie looked down at her crumpled dress, making a face.

'She was in a hurry today, right beta? Okay, I must go now, the kitchen needs my attention. You kids have a good time.'

Her job done, the aunty graced her with a look as if to say don't-let-me-down-young-lady and departed, leaving behind a whiff of her perfume and a whole lot of awkward silence.

She never did well with silences, so she began to babble.

'That's a lie. I don't cook anything. At all. And I don't go to the gym. I hate working out. I sweat too much.'

He stared at her. She kept talking. 'I swim and do yoga . . . Sometimes . . . Not every day . . .' She let out a nervous laugh.

Anal remained expressionless.

An awkward silence reigned yet again.

'So I hear you're a doctor. What do you specialize in?'

She looked at his face. *It really was a cute face.* Light eyes, full lips, nice jaw. Kind of like Ranbir Kapoor, but a plump, tall, teddy bear version.

She decided to make the best of the situation, so she smiled prettily and started flirting with him.

'Wait, wait! Don't tell me, let me guess.'

'Um, okay.'

'Surgeon?'

'No.'

'Cardiologist?'

'No.'

'Paediatrician?'

'No.'

'Nutritionist?'

'No.'

'Dentist?!'

'No.'

'I give up! But whatever it is, I promise I'll go only to you from now on and recommend you to all my friends and family.'

He gave her a tight smile, 'I'm a gynaecologist.'

'Oh!' Anal spelled ANAL was a gynaecologist.

Before she could think of something to say, Aunt Perizad announced that the cake was being cut. This gave them both the perfect excuse to flee.

Once assembled, Anal's father, Mr Malhotra, who was drunk, raised his glass to the room. Everyone followed suit.

Mr Malhotra slurred, 'I would like to raise a toast! To my son, Anal, and this pretty girl. Beti, do you know I've known your parents since I was a boy? And you've known Anal since you were a girl. You and Anal used to run around naked together and, of course, I did the same with your mum.'

An audible gasp and several scandalized murmurs made their way around the room.

Anal's mother, Mrs Malhotra, shot her husband a stern look. She must have been around fifty-five but was desperately trying to pull a thirty in a black leather skirt and a white blouse that was a couple of sizes too small for what seemed like a thirty-eight-inch chest size.

Oblivious to his wife's glare, the intoxicated man continued, 'Our families know each other now for three generations, even our grandparents were friends. Maybe they also ran together naked as kids.' He let out a big roaring laugh and then gulped his whiskey as he noticed his wife giving him a look.

Anal's grandmother looked up from her wheelchair at her son.

'I was never naked,' she primly stated.

Mr Malhotra, clearly used to ignoring the women of his house, barrelled on. Picking up an oyster from the table and slurping it noisily, he exclaimed, 'Good for virility!'

The aunties followed suit. Anal made his way towards her. She didn't know what to do so she uncomfortably picked up an oyster from the table and offered it to him. He took it from her and popped it into his mouth, the juices flying from his mouth on to her face. *Quite intimate for a first meeting,* she thought.

'So I say cheers to generations of friendship between the families and here's to it finally turning into . . .' He then fixed his gaze on Anal and her.

'Something *more* than friendship.'

Everybody at the party followed his gaze and obediently raised their glasses in unison. *Something more than friendship!* Before she could wonder what he meant by that, a skinny middle-aged man blew out the birthday candles, causing the room to echo with loud applause.

Once the chaos died down, she immediately made her way to Aunty Perizad.

'This is so weird. I can't believe you did this to ME, aunty.'

'What are you complaining about? He is so nice, so handsome, so polite,' she said.

'Aunty, his name is *Anal.* Spelled ANAL. Imagine that on our wedding card. My friends will never let me forget it.'

'I don't see why that matters, he's a gynaecologist, a well-respected one at that.'

Is that all it takes? This is what Aunty thinks is on the list of what I want in a man?

1. Well-respected gynaecologist. Check.

'Aunty, I can't be with a guy called Anal who spends all day with his face between women's legs. Gross.'

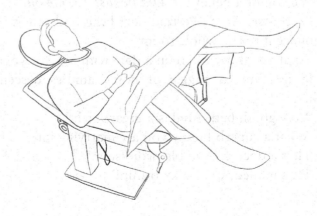

'Beggars can't be choosers, beti. You are quite old now.'

Did she just call me a beggar? And OLD? I'm twenty-three. 'And by the way, single doesn't mean desperate. It means I am focusing on my career, personal growth and happiness.'

Aunty Perizad wasn't even listening.

'This is ridiculous. I'm leaving.' She turned around, only to come face to face with Anal who was standing right behind her the entire time.

Oh shit.

She stood there, embarrassed, wishing for the ground to open up and swallow her whole. She looked at his retreating back, still within earshot, and muttered a meek bye.

He unexpectedly stopped, turned around and marched purposefully back towards her. He handed her a flier. 'You said you like yoga?'

'I go every Friday.'

He nodded and resumed his earlier walk to the door. She looked at the flier: Hot Yoga.

She couldn't believe it. *Did he just ask me out?*

Of course, Aunty Perizad heard this and saw it fit to announce it to the whole room.

'Anal asked her to go on a date with him for yoga!'

In no time, a gaggle of nosey aunties descended on her.

'Very good, beti. Anal is a great catch.'

'What a superb family you are marrying into.'

'He's a doctor. A noble profession.'

'He's loaded, you lucky tramp!'

'Better practise his favourite dishes.'

'We have a wedding to plan!'

They all giggled and began chatting animatedly about the wedding. All this talk overwhelmed her. She excused herself. Making her way to the table, she picked a batata vada. Her first bite, however, was interrupted by the women who were planning the wedding. They looked at her in horror and screamed in eerie unison, 'DON'T EAT THAT!'

Yoga Class: That Friday Evening

The class was in session and she entered late wearing a brand new bright pink yoga outfit.

She spotted Anal sitting in the middle of the class dressed in full black, eyes closed and legs crossed in the lotus position. She clumsily navigated herself towards him, squeezing herself between Anal and a very annoyed woman.

The yoga teacher paced the room slowly.

'Inhale one, two, three, four and hold . . .' he instructed.

She took a deep breath and quickly glanced over at Anal, who still had his eyes closed. *Mmmm . . . cute face. If he can turn the fat into muscle then maybe . . .*

'Now exhale two, three, four . . .'

She peeped at Anal again. 'Girl in pink, close your eyes,' the yoga teacher yelled. 'Breathe breathe, girl in pink,' the yoga teacher said.

As she did so, an image of Anal and her making out popped into her head.

Her eyes flew open. *That was weird.*

The yoga teacher tapped her shoulder again.

'Eyes closed, deep breaths.'

She took an enormous deep breath, almost choking. The yoga teacher tapped her shoulder *again*.

She opened her eyes to find that everyone was on their feet, doing surya namaskar.

Embarrassed, she followed suit, exhaling really loudly. This attracted a lot of stares. Cringing, she shot the onlookers an apologetic look.

Kind of strange. Asking ME for a date to a yoga class. Not very intimate, she thought as she saw Anal move in front of her.

Everyone shifted to the downward dog position.

Anal's butt and her face were too close for comfort. *On second thought, maybe a little too intimate.*

The teacher had changed the pose to a headstand. She clumsily switched too. From her upside down position, she turned to look at Anal, who was now again beside her.

He met her eyes. 'You're flexible.'

'Thanks.'

She shut her eyes. Immediately another image of them making out popped up in her head.

Ewwww!!!! What's wrong with ME? I never like plump guys. Maybe I am about to get my period. PMSing does make me want to get with everyone.

She closed her eyes. An image of him shirtless, hairy with a belly popped up and she imagined her hand running down his belly. She lost control. These distractions were too much. Her back bent and she went down, her legs swinging. On her journey downwards, her heel met with Anal's face. Anal yelped and held his nose.

'Oh. Sorry. God, I'm so sorry!' Anal cupped his profusely bleeding nose as the yoga teacher rushed to him.

'Are you okay? Is it broken?'

'I-I'm fine. I'll be fine.'

He turned away from the instructor and hurried towards the door, holding his face up so the blood didn't drip. She ran after him.

'Anal, I'm so sorry! I'm such a . . .

Anal left, leaving her standing there in her brand-new, bright pink yoga outfit, feeling terrible.

Recipe

Oysters, good for virility

LESSON LEARNT

1. Stay away from aunties while in your twenties and stay away from boys when PMSing.

2. Downward dog with a guy named ANAL is a bad idea.

3. Arranged marriage is like a perfectly written recipe handed down through generations but one surprise ingredient can just ruin it all.

WHERE IS HE NOW?

Anal is still a bachelor, living in South Mumbai. He's a very well-known gynaecologist, and his waiting room is always packed with pregnant women from all over Mumbai.

THREE THANK YOU'S AND A SORRY

1. She thanks him for inviting her to the yoga class.

2. She thanks him for being so polite even after she was quite rude.

3. She thanks him for being a gentleman.

She is sorry she kicked him in the face and broke his nose.

11

Is There Any Logic in Love?

Cupid had struck her hormones. She was in a love trance. Happy hormones flooded her body and brain every time she saw him. Fuelled by dopamine, she felt ecstatic around him and just couldn't seem to get enough.

What she saw through her rose-tinted, love-struck eyes: broad shoulders, a great butt, big pouty lips (basically a younger version of Brad Pitt) with jet black shiny hair.

What the reality was: Skinny, gelled hair, very white skin, too much cologne and a really interesting nose.

Beauty indeed lies in the eyes of the beholder. She had her first drink with him.

She went to all the Bombay parties for the first time with him.

She smoked her first doob with him.

She went to fancy restaurants for the first time with him.

She drove his car (which happened to be a BMW) all the way from Town to Bandra for the first time with him.

They were different. He was the kind that hated walking on the beach because he couldn't stand sand in his shoes. She loved walking barefoot in the sand, grass and anywhere possible.

But they found their differences funny. He called her Nature Girl. She called him Vodka Boy. They made jokes about it.

Her parents didn't approve, not because of his looks but because he came from a family that didn't have a great reputation.

They called him Frankenstein.

Her friends, Malini and Jarna, were wary of him.

'He's shady.'

'He parties too much.'

'He cheated on his ex.'

'He lies.'

Their warnings rang in her ears, but she ignored them all.

There was just something about him. He was smooth, charming and made her laugh and giggle.

He loved strawberry ice cream. They often found themselves in Naturals licking ice cream together, giggling at his jokes.

She travelled for the first time in her life to Europe. A solo backpacking trip. But after a few weeks he started missing her and showed up at her dorm.

They went to Italy and Switzerland. And while she wanted to see everything, he just wanted to chill, but somehow they found a balance and giggled all the way about how different they were. They laughed a lot.

All his jokes were funny until a year later, when the feel-good hormones and brain chemicals were starting to return to normal, and she suddenly began to notice little things. He drank way too much and his drunk rambling, which was once adorable, had become increasingly confusing. He had a myriad other habits that she couldn't help noticing. It was a broad spectrum that ranged from blatantly flirting with girls in front of her to fights instigated by him on Fridays that lasted the weekend after which they'd find their way back to this bubble of infatuation by Sunday. In this bubble, he was still so attractive, still made her laugh and they still travelled, ate a lot of strawberry ice cream and had a lot of fun together.

And that's the thing about attraction; it can blind you to everything else and throw caution to the wind.

She was in the studio hosting her 1000th episode on MTV. It was a big day and a great number of people had tuned in. She was on the couch, taking questions. She called on a girl from the live audience who had raised her hand.

'Hi, I'm Jugnoo. Don't you think it's still a male-dominated world out here in India?'

She considered the question. With a deep breath she replied, 'Hi Jugnoo. Well, um . . . Yes. I think that it's a male-dominated world if we let it be. I mean, the world is the world we *let* it be, but we can make it the world we *want* it to be.'

Meanwhile, on the other end of the screen, her best friends were watching her from a beauty parlour. Jarna was getting a head massage and munching on potato wedges drenched in mayo with her big belly (she was pregnant at the time), and a very sad, tired looking Yogi, who had just broken up with her boyfriend, was getting her legs waxed.

'Indian women face challenges, we all know that. We may feel boxed in by customs and fears and expectations. But we should be allowed to reject those things if they aren't . . . right for us.'

In the beauty parlour, Yogi yelped as a strip of wax was pulled from her leg.

At the same time, in her living room, her parents, sister and a group of aunties were watching too.

The aunties all beamed with pride when they heard her say, 'My own loving, beautiful mother looks at my world, my choices and my possibilities, and it's a world she doesn't even recognize. Our generation of women have the opportunity to create a world that isn't, as you say, male dominated. And I believe we can.'

On hearing her speak, one of the aunties was compelled to share her own pearl of wisdom: 'She sounds like she's lost weight.'

The live audience clapped, and the switchboard lit up. It was time. 'All right, let's go to a call. We're on with . . .' she announced as she read from the screen. A muffled voice responded on the other end, the words not quite audible. She looked over at the control booth. The confused engineer held his hands up behind the glass panel.

'Hi, you are on air.'

Suddenly, the muffled voice responded. It was positively female, and it said, 'TV GIRL, stop seeing him.'

Her eyes widened.

Confused and wary, she ventured in an amiable voice, 'Sorry? Do you have a question for me?'

The muffled female voice on the other end hesitated. 'He . . . is with you and me, and God knows how many others for God knows how many months.'

In her home living room, her parents, sister and the aunties were all shocked.

'Frankenstein?' her sister screeched.

Back at the studio, she let out an uncomfortable laugh. *This must be some sort of prank.* 'Nice one, guys. Very funny. Jarna, is that you? I'm gonna get you for this, you fat, pregnant monster.' With forced humour, she began making silly monster voices, trying to alleviate the tension.

In the beauty parlour, Jarna had stopped eating. Nobody was laughing.

The tone of the muffled female voice grew sharper, 'If you don't believe me, I'm dialling his number right now.' The sound of a phone ringing followed. She listened carefully as did the rest of Mumbai. There was a rapid montage in her brain of various people from different walks of life watching the show. College kids gathered around the TV. A tobacco seller turning up his small TV. A maid sweeping the floor pausing to watch. *This better be a joke.*

And then, Frankenstein answered the phone. 'Hello?'

The muffled female said, 'Hi, lover boy. It's ME.'

His response was devastatingly instantaneous. 'Hey. You coming over?'

'But what about your girlfriend, that TV girl?'

'Listen babe, I've told you before, I HAVE NO GIRLFRIEND. Now, you coming or not? Wear that black dress I got you from Switzerland.'

'Okay. See you later.' The line went silent. She sat in the studio, confused, angry, humiliated.

But the muffled female voice had more to say. 'Oh and TV girl, one last thing.'

'What?'

'He gave me HPV. You better get yourself checked out right away.' The phone line went dead. She sat there shocked, her eyes brimming with tears.

The live audience started talking.

As she moved to rush out of the studio, she encountered her boss. He was positively joyous.

'Great show. Highest ratings ever!'

She side stepped him and ran out of the office crying. Her phone rang. Unknown number. 'Hello?'

'Sorry that I had to do that on TV,' said the same muffled female voice.

'What? How do you have my number?'

'Let me take you to my gynaecologist for a check-up to make this up to you.'

'No, thank you.'

'I am not the enemy, TV girl,' she tried to reason. 'He is. He did this. I didn't.'

Later, she found herself sitting in the waiting room of the gynaecologist's office, holding hands with the girl with the muffled voice. Muffled Voice was short, very fair, with giant boobs and bleached blonde hair, like all those rich South Mumbai girls have.

She was miserable. Her eyes were puffy, her hair a mess and her clothes were wrinkled. Muffled Voice Girl, on the other hand, was wearing a short skirt with boots. Her hair was blow-dried and her make-up was intact.

'I'm from Pedder Road, South Mumbai,' she stated. She had a strawberry ice cream cone in her hand that she was licking very suggestively.

Strawberry ice cream. That is my thing with Frankenstein. And why is she eating the ice cream like that? Does she wish the best for me or the worst? I feel like throwing up.

'It's the best clinic in the city. I love this doctor,' Muffled Voice Girl said. *Why was she being so nice to me?*

The strawberry ice cream was melting. Some spilled on her boobs. Muffled Voice Girl laughed. Joys of having huge boobs, she said as she suggestively wiped it.

Her eyes started to tear up. Her boobs felt like little tennis balls compared to Muffled Voice Girl's football boobs.

The receptionist came out from behind her desk. 'Are you that TV girl?'

She was tempted to deny such an allegation, claiming familial similarity to the cousin who was the TV girl. But it seemed like too much work. Embarrassed, she simply nodded.

The receptionist smiled, gestured and led her in. While walking towards the office she whispered, 'If you want that piece-of-shit boyfriend taken care of, I know some people.'

She almost considered the offer, but 'muffled voice' was by her side.

'Do you mind just waiting here? I mean. You can even go home. You've done enough. Thank you!'

'I am absolutely not leaving. We are in this together. I will wait here if it makes you feel more comfortable.'

Hearing this, she simply sighed and entered the examination room.

Moments later, she lay on a table wearing a green plastic robe, embarrassed and uncomfortable. A nurse lifted her legs high and straddled them into stirrups. The doors swung open and the gynaecologist entered. There was a curtain between them. She couldn't see him and he couldn't see her. She just lay still, her eyes shut tight.

She heard him putting on surgical gloves and then he began the examination. He started speaking to her from between her legs. 'Routine check-up?'

'Well, actually, no. I just found out that my boyfriend . . . has another girlfriend. Maybe more than one.' Admitting this made her cry. The nurse passed a tissue pitifully. She blew her nose loudly. 'And one of them . . . he gave one of them HPV!'

The doctor stiffened subtly on his side of the curtain. 'We'll check it out.'

He put his head back down. She saw him reach out for a big scary instrument and this proved to be the cataclysmic trigger to emotions. She screamed. The nurse took her hand in her firm, comforting grasp and the doctor said, 'Relax. Breathe.'

She started breathing fast, irregular breaths that made her sound as if she were in the throes of labour.

'Relax, relax. Deep breaths with me.' The doctor tried to breathe deeply but he instead started wheezing loudly. There must be something wrong with his nose.

'Done. Done. All done.' He swivelled and rolled across the floor on his stool towards a microscope, his back towards her.

'So? What is it?' she asked tentatively. His face was still covered, and he was looking into the scope.

'Hmmm . . . mmm . . .' he hummed noncommittally.

'Do I have it?'

'Hmmm . . . mmm . . .' Again, with the humming.

'Doctor?'

'No. No. You are safe,' he finally said.

He continued to look at her file.

'You are lucky, though. I suggest you stop having random, promiscuous sex.'

'No, it was one guy, my boyfriend, or at least I thought he was my boyfriend!' she found herself becoming defensive.

Wheeling his stool back beside the examination table, he advised, 'And please, henceforth, perform any and all sexual activity with protection.' He pulled off the surgical gloves and pushed the plastic curtain down and found himself face to face with her.

Ahhhhh! They both screamed loudly!

Of all the clinics in the world, she had walked into his!

His nose throbbed, remembering the damage her heel had done to it.

Anal collected himself quickly.

'Hello.' She was too busy trying to frantically cover herself to reply. Anal didn't know what to do or say. He looked everywhere. He then finally spoke, fixing his gaze on the wall. 'Um . . . Thank you. Okay. Goodbye. You are clean. VERY CLEAN. And nice.'

He quickly exited the room. She burst into tears.

Nice?

Muffled Voice Girl ran in, her boobs jumping up and down, hitting her face in slow motion.

'Are you okay? Let's go to Naturals and get some strawberry ice cream.'

RECIPE

Strawberry ice cream

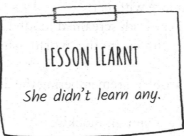

LESSON LEARNT

She didn't learn any.

Frankenstein makes it to the next chapter.

12.

DID YOU NEED DISTANCE TO BRING YOU CLOSER?

She had just faced the biggest humiliation of her life. There was no joy for her in her TV show any more. She was heartbroken over Frankenstein and felt embarrassment every day when people asked her about him. She wanted to run away and hide.

And so, she decided to break her piggy bank and every bank, take all her savings and fly to New York City where she knew nobody. She enrolled in an acting course. She was going to start a new life.

In which other city in the world can you walk on the street and openly cry without anyone even glancing at you?

Welcome to the summer of 2001 in New York City!

It was June when she first stepped on American soil. She firmly decided that Frankenstein was a thing of the past and New York her future.

Free concerts in Central Park, museums, art galleries and a whole lot of Craigslist apartments (this was pre-Airbnb).

Eye contact with hot strangers in the streets, conversations with mysterious boys at bars. This was pre-online dating, when guys talked to you at bars and restaurants.

She was tasting cuisines she had never tried before—Korean, African, Jamaican, Puerto Rican. She was on an adventure! Frankenstein with his big nose and gelled hair was slowly becoming a blur. She had been there three months and she had no intention of going back although her savings were slowly running out.

She was writing applications to be a waitress while her boss from the TV station kept emailing her. She didn't want to go back but the restaurants were rejecting her because she had no previous waitressing experience and she didn't even have a Green Card.

But that did not stop her from being excited that day. She had a walk date in Central Park with a hot black guy with long dreadlocks who looked exactly like Lenny Kravitz (but taller).

What should she wear? She squeezed into the leather skirt she had bought in a thrift shop.

The buzzer of her tiny East Village apartment rang abruptly. Who could that be in the middle of the afternoon?

She opened the door to find Frankenstein standing there!

He flashed her a sexy half grin.

'Can I come in?'

She was in shock, she stared at him.

Laying on the charm, Frankenstein said, 'I flew 8000 miles to return this to you,' and handed her a copy of *Men Are From Mars*.

There was a long pause. She couldn't believe her eyes.

Then, she mumbled, 'I've never seen that book before except in a bookshop.'

'Oh, it's not yours?' Frankenstein was trying to sound surprised.

'NO.'

'Now it is,' he replied cheekily. 'Aren't you going to invite me in?'

She handed the book back to him.

'I don't want this! How on earth did you find me?'

'What guy ever flew 8000 miles to return a book to you?'

'That's not even my book! And you still haven't answered my question.'

Did he Google Earth her before Dev Patel's character Google Earthed his mother? Or did a loud-mouthed common friend blurt out her new address to him?

All the same, she couldn't help blushing. There was something special about him and it was flattering that he had flown all the way to see her. He winked and pushed himself in.

She was charmed. Was it his big nose, his big lips, his popping eyes or just his swag? Frankenstein had swag before the word 'swag' was even a thing. And she was a sucker for swag. If she wasn't, it would have saved her a whole lot of time but then she wouldn't have all these recipes to share.

He pushed past her into her cute little apartment and walked straight into her house mates' room.

'Hey, wait, wait . . . that's not my room . . .' she ran behind him.

'You share?' he asked, completely mortified.

'Yes, of course. How else could I afford an apartment in East Village?'

'Come home,' he said.

She paused. HOME?

'This is home.'

'I'm sorry, you have to live in this little ratty place. Is this your room? Oh gosh, you don't even have a door, just a curtain . . .' he said inspecting her room.

'Actually I love my little room with "just a curtain".'

The front door opened abruptly. Her house mate, who was one half of the couple she roomed with, entered.

'Hi Greg. This is . . .'

'What's up!' Greg hi-fived her and walked into his room without even looking up.

Frankenstein stopped speaking and went red in the face.

'You live with a guy?'

'No.'

'But that was a guy.'

'I live with two guys. Greg and Tom.'

'What?'

'I'm not sleeping with them. And anyway, they wouldn't be interested in sleeping with me, even if I were. They're a couple. Anyway, what on earth are you doing here, asking me all these questions?'

Frankenstein had grown very quiet.

He walked into her room and just sat on her bed.

'This is terrible. You don't even have a real bed!' he lamented.

'It's a very comfortable mattress.'

'Look,' she said, opening the window. 'It's not all bad, I can see the Twin Towers from my apartment.'

He came to the window. 'That's a beautiful view of the World Trade Center,' he said and added, 'But I miss you.'

He said this with such earnestness that she felt her heart melt.

'Come home with me.'

'I . . . I . . . that's very romantic . . . but I'm not sure if I'm ready to . . .'

He pulled her close and kissed her passionately. She pulled away.

'This is crazy. I shouldn't . . . You treated me badly.'

'I was an idiot. Sorry. Can't you forgive me?' And saying so, he kissed her again. 'He cheated on you. Can you have a relationship without trust?' her inner voice warned.

Just then, Greg called out to her. *Ugh! Bad timing.* She excused herself and went to the common room.

'You left your towel on the floor again.'

'I'm sorry. I've just been so caught up. And my ex from India suddenly showed up and . . .'

'Hey girl, your boyfriends are YOUR problem, not mine.'

She apologized and hurried back into the room. *Sigh! Americans! Or was it New Yorkers? Or just Greg?*

When she came back, she saw Frankenstein tying his shoelaces.

'Where are you going?'

'I'm leaving . . .'

'What? Why?'

Frankenstein opened his palm and showed her something . . . It was a condom. She had a little collection right on her bed side table as a joke. In a fishbowl.

'Am I supposed to explain that?' she questioned.

'So you're seeing someone?' he counter questioned.

'I was . . . He's a really nice guy. But it's over now.'

'How many of those did you use?'

'Why am I explaining myself to you? You came here to apologize to me.'

'How many times did you use these?'

'Actually, none.'

He stared at her with tears in his eyes. It was all so bizarre. The guy who humiliated her on TV in front of the entire country was now standing in front of her with tears in his eyes. *Oh, how the tides turn.*

'Nobody actually uses those NYC condoms. They are given out for free at restaurants as a joke and are not really good. I'd rather buy real condoms. You know Trojan is pretty popular here.'

'You have changed.' And saying so, he walked out.

'Come on, don't leave . . .'

She pulled him back into the room.

'He couldn't do it . . .' she said. 'We tried . . . he er . . . had a little problem . . . he smoked too much stuff and his thing just did not go up, so we decided to be just friends . . .'

He stared at her in disbelief.

'I am not lying. But really even if I did do it, you have no right to come here and demand an explanation.'

'I'm sorry I came to get you. I see you have moved on. I am leaving.'

She ran to her wardrobe, pulled out a big black vibrator and threw it at Frankenstein.

'Catch,' she said. He caught it.

'What the eff is this?'

'He gave this to me.'

'This is huge!'

'I know. It's also my first vibrator. He should have got me something smaller.'

'This is disgusting,' he remarked and threw it back at her.

She caught it.

'Who are these men you are meeting who give you these . . . things?' he asked, looking at the vibrator with disgust.

'He's a nice guy. He couldn't do it, so he gave me that. You know, as a compensation.'

'But you still tried to do it.'

'Yeah, so what? We were not even in touch. You almost gave me HPV.'

'The HPV was a lie. I don't have it.'

He threw the vibrator back at her and marched off, out of the apartment.

'Wait! What do you mean it was a lie?'

She chased him down the street like a scene straight out of a Hindi movie. People stared at her. She didn't realize she was still holding the big black thing.

She followed him all the way to the W Hotel in Mid Town.

When they entered his room, he grabbed the vibrator from her, threw it in the trash can and kissed her hard.

'I forgive you,' he murmured in her ear, breaking the kiss.

Huh?

Confused, she just smiled. After all he had flown 8000 miles to surprise her.

'How can you prove you don't have HPV?'

'We can go for a test now.'

And they did. And it turned out he was clear. He went down on his knees and asked her to marry him outside the hospital they had taken the test in. She was overwhelmed with emotion, and even though there was no ring, she said yes.

After which, they had a great little weekend in New York. They ate New York cheesecake in bed, watched plays, walked about museums, went dancing. She was once again IN LOVE!

On his last night in NY, as he packed his bag, he whispered to her, 'The ring is coming on Tuesday.'

She blushed . . .

'You're going to have to wait for six months, mister. I'm not coming back to India right away. I have to finish my course and my money.' She laughed.

Once he left, she went back to her little apartment with a twinkle in her eye. She called up all her friends and told them there was a ring coming on Tuesday.

'Is it going to be a destination wedding?' they all asked excitedly.

She giggled.

The Lenny Kravitz double was texting her, she texted back, 'I am so sorry I stood you up. You're so hot but I am getting married. Yes, I know, very unexpected. Sorry. I'm sure you have a line of girls.'

Tuesday came and went. She had not heard from Frankenstein in over a week's time. He wasn't even answering her calls. He had ghosted her before ghosting was even a thing.

Two weeks later, as she sat on her mattress, staring morosely at the NYC condoms, she got a call from her friend Kinari.

'I'm sorry to be the bearer of bad news, but Frankenstein has been spotted many, many times with Muffled Voice Girl.'

'What? Why are you telling me this now?' she exclaimed.

'Well, nobody wanted to tell you because . . .'

'I thought you were my friend.'

Greg poked his head in her room through the curtain.

'Can you keep it down, please? We're trying to sleep here.'

'Sorry. Why am I the last to know?'

Greg peeped in again.

'Sorry! Sorry!' she said to him.

God, Americans! Could they be less anal, at least when I am going through a crisis? My marriage is falling apart before I even got properly engaged. And he wants me to 'keep it down'?

'I saw him yesterday at the Fire and Ice nightclub. And he was carrying her bag!' Kinari said.

'*Her bag?*' she screamed again.

'That's when I decided I must tell you.'

Carrying another woman's handbag! That was a sure shot deal breaker, her inner monologue screamed.

'You were doing so well in New York before he showed up. Take care. Go back to whatever you were doing before he came,' Kinari said.

She hung up and looked at her watch. It was 1 a.m.

She let out another scream, sobbing loudly.

Greg barged into her room, screaming, 'God, woman! We have to go to work tomorrow. Can we please catch up on some sleep?'

She officially hated the cheap thin walls in America, OH WAIT, there were no walls, just a curtain. Frankenstein was right, she was slumming it.

She counted on her fingers. It was around 11 a.m. in India.

Please note: These were the days before Skype or WhatsApp calls. Before international phone calls became cheap. She was spending Rs 10,000 on a call. Rs 10,000! That was a lot especially when she had busted through more than half of all her savings already.

She called up Frankenstein and surprisingly he picked up in one ring.

She blurted the question out through tears.

'Were you with Muffled Voice at Fire and Ice?'

He paused. And then spoke solemnly.

'Yes.'

'You were holding her purse?'

'You had a bowl of condoms in your apartment.'

'How is that even relevant?'

'I can't get over it.'

'But we were not together then . . .'

'You keep saying that like it means something.'

'You love Muffled Voice?'

'We have become very close.'

'In two weeks?'

He said nothing.

'And the ring?'

'What ring?'

She hung up, red in the face.

Greg marched into her room just then.

'I'm sorry but we've been meaning to tell you. You need to move out.'

She looked up at him through tears, her face smudged with mascara.

'Your lease is up, and we can't extend. You've been crying a lot recently. You just look depressed and it's not a good look. You are too loud on the phone.'

'I'm sorry . . . I'm sorry. I will try to keep it down,' she pleaded with him.

'Not just that. It's your food . . .'

'I'm sorry I know I am not the best cook. I won't insist on you eating it if you hate my cooking. It's just that in India, we offer our food . . .'

'It's the smell . . .'

'Smell?'

'The smell of curry. The whole house reeks of it the day you cook something Indian.'

'Who doesn't love the smell of curry? It's the one thing that makes life better when your boyfriend dumps you for the second time for a woman with football-sized boobs. In fact I want to eat some now.'

'You have to leave.'

'Because of my curry?'

'Everything is yellow.'

'Huh? You have something against the colour?'

'There's turmeric in everything. Even your eggs have turmeric. I'm sick of having a yellow kitchen. The whole house smells of curry. If you don't cook it, you get curry take out. Every day, its curry.'

'But . . .' He walked out. She chased him.

'I. . . . I won't cook. I won't get curry home . . . I . . . I . . . can I at least eat a little curry now? One last time? I'm in a really bad place right now.'

'Our decision is final. We have someone moving in next week, so please find somewhere else.'

The next day, she woke up with a start. Greg and Tom were in her room, pulling the window open. She saw smoke coming out of the Twin Towers.

She sat up in bed. 'What is happening?'

BOOM! The towers collapsed right in front of her eyes.

Recipe

A banging yellow curry

LESSON LEARNT

1. If he betrayed you once, he will most likely betray you again.

2. Some boys just bring out the pathetic little needy victim in us. Those are the boys to stay away from.

3. Cheaters are like a wine stain on your favourite white dress that will never come out.

4. Discovering you have been betrayed for the second time by the same guy feels like the aftertaste of Stevia in your favourite dessert. It stays with you for a long time.

WHERE IS HE NOW?

Frankenstein in now a proud father of two girls and lives right across her apartment in Bandra. They run into each other on the street.

THREE THANK YOU'S AND A SORRY:

1. She thanks him for the Copa Cabana, Ghetto and Frangipaani memories!

2. She thanks him for making her laugh till her stomach hurt.

3. She thanks him for buying her the first air conditioner she ever had. Yeah, they had none in the house till he gifted her one.

She can't think of anything to say sorry about.

SHE MISSES:

1. His stupid laugh. It was cute.

2. His big nose that he never let her touch.

3. Him teasing her and calling her Nature Girl.

13

Do We Chase 'Bad Boys' because they Free Us from the Pressure of Being 'Good Girls'?

On 31 October 2001, she, a new healing version of herself, bounced into Ricky's. She had decided to renounce men and concentrate on her career. Ricky's was an edgy, ultra-hip beauty shop that came alive with wigs and costumes during Halloween.

She was there to shoot a pilot for her first self-produced travel show.

This was a big risk with her last bit of savings but it was all or nothing!

She had a plan, shoot a show in New York which would drain her of every penny of her savings and then, she would take it to TV channels in India as a sample. She hoped that they would love it and they would fund her for her own travel show on TV, after which she would travel around the world!

In the middle of the first take, her eyes tripped over the man behind the camera. He was an exceptionally tall, lean but muscular man with a big afro and a prominent black mole on the right side of his face.

His skin was caramel and his nose was painted red (for Halloween). It was adoration at first sight. Her usual shyness around men she found attractive was superseded by the outrageous courage the focus of the camera gave her.

'Wow, my cameraman is so cute, I'm going to lean in for a kiss.' A bold move, one she would have never made if the camera wasn't on. Somehow the camera always helped her lose her fears and be bolder than she was. She leaned in. He bent down grinning and smack, he pecked her on the lips. An electric current went through her. He winked. 'You're not so bad yourself,' he said in the sexiest voice she had ever heard.

He moved behind the camera like he was gliding in air. *Wait! He's wearing skates.* He was on roller blades that added what seemed like four inches to his six feet frame. 'I've never seen a cameraman on skates,' she stated. 'Stick with me, babe. There are a lot of things I can show you that you've never seen.' She felt herself sweating. God! He was HOT.

They belonged to very different worlds—she was from Bandra, Mumbai, he was from the Bronx, New York. The Bronx is one of the roughest neighbourhoods in New York, known for gangs, murders, car thefts, shootings and burglaries.

All she knew about the Bronx then was from the Jenifer Lopez song, 'I'm Just Jenny From The Bronx'.

He introduced her to a whole new world. Skate parks and underground hip hop clubs where he would just start jamming with his hip hopper friends.

Brooklyn and Harlem, in those days, were sexy, dangerous and exhilarating! Just like him.

This was 2001 when New York was still cool and not run by rich, Wall Street types. Or maybe it was, and they just didn't notice.

They met often, shooting her self-funded show together. He told her she didn't need to pay him, just share the profits! Perfect.

He was showing her a whole different side to New York, one she would never have access to without him. Her show was going to be so cool! He was so cool.

She forgot about Frankenstein and was enthralled by this sexy, young, cool, pro-athlete, skateboarder and rollerblader. She went to his shows where he would jump off twenty-feet ramps. He was so smooth! But she was not the only woman who thought so. He had a lot of fans, female fans.

She and the rest of the girls watched in awe as he did his tricks on skates. If he fell, he'd just laugh and brush it off and wink at her. 'Doesn't it hurt?' she asked seeing the blood pouring out from his knee. He laughed and wiped it off with the back of his hand. 'That's just a cut, babe,' he said in his sexy Bronx accent. She was weak in the knees.

'He is no ordinary skateboarder. He is actually famous in that world. Young kids come up and ask for a picture. He has been on the cover of some skating magazines,' she told her friend Sonia. 'Did he even go to school?' Sonia cross questioned. 'He's a kid from the streets. The Bronx is the UP and Bihar of New York.'

'I can't help it,' she said. 'He's like a drug.'

Sonia, who only liked the banker type, rolled her eyes.

'This skating thing is his job? Can he even pay for lunch?'

'I don't care,' she said firmly.

Sometimes, when women came up and giggled and touched him and took pictures with him, she felt a strong tinge of jealousy. She tried to brush it off, just like he brushed off his bruises.

Sometimes he'd lift her up in front of all the girls and put her on his skateboard; she would hold on tight, and they'd gallivant around the city. She felt so cool.

This was better than being in any car. Porsches and BMWs went by, but she was blissful with him on that skateboard.

And so the romance began with this very attractive boy-man on roller blades. There was no need to go on exploratory dates with him; the chemistry was live and tangible and instantaneous.

That bad boy charm, oozing testosterone, bold and so hot!

There were red flags; she could see them right up front. He was just so charming with every woman, flirted with every waitress or fan and had a grandiose view of himself as he signed autographs for younger skater kids. But she was smitten; red flags felt like red bangles.

She couldn't explain the connection.

It wasn't even that he was the most handsome man she had seen.

Was it the half-smile, his big curly afro hair, his voice, his accent?

Or maybe, he was the kid in Puerto Rico in nappies who had hit her on the head with a bat when she was three.

Or maybe she was just drawn to his impulsive behaviour and bad boy energy.

She had no idea what it was, but it felt good, and she felt happy just by looking at him.

Sometimes she'd get upset about him giving some girl too much attention or flirting back or offering some exotic woman a lollipop but then he'd take her to eat mofongo, a Puerto Rican dish with fried plantains and garlic as its main ingredient, and all would be forgotten as they would eat from the same bowl.

He once came to meet her while she was with her friends, Sonia and Ruvani.

He rolled into the bar on skates with his beanie on, sucking on his trademark lollipop.

'Show the girls your hair,' she said to him proudly and he took off his beanie. Out jumped his beautiful curly afro.

Ruvani let out a little scream.

She laughed, enjoying shocking her friends who went for those finance dudes.

'What does she, a girl from India, have in common with this dangerous-looking guy from the Bronx with a huge afro who never takes off his skates and sucks lollipops?' they argued but she just laughed them off.

She was so into him!

He wasn't the most reliable either. He was almost half an hour late for every date, and when she asked where he'd been, he'd give her a cute half smile and say, 'Girl, I was doing my thing.' This made her laugh. 'Your thing? What's your thing?'

His replies would always be nonchalant but she thought it was adorable until one of his friends casually mentioned they skated around New York carrying marijuana in their backpacks, delivering it to the Wall Street types.

That was his thing?

She tried to ask him about it, but he smoothly changed the subject. She didn't push it.

He was supposed to be the camera person for her pilot but she found herself always capturing him on her DSLR camera as he'd glide in and out of her world.

One day he left her home in the morning. They had been out all night, in underground hip hop bars. Hot black dudes rapped free style while he and his friends skated around on ramps. Then they went around at night making wild graffiti art with spray paint on the walls of Brooklyn. Her mind was blown. She was finally part of the cool gang! That afternoon he called her. 'Hello. Hi. I just wanted to say hi,' he said and hung up.

She didn't see him for two days after that. When she did, he casually mentioned he had called her from jail. 'WHAT!?' He said it was nothing serious, he had jumped over the subway turnstile and the police had caught him and put him in jail for a night.

But even that didn't faze her. It made him more attractive. He was so exciting, dangerous and forbidden.

'And I was flattered I was his one phone call from jail!' she told her friends Sonia and Ruvani, who couldn't understand her obsession with this guy.

'Aren't you going back to India? What will happen then?'

She shrugged.

'You just want his bad boy sperm, not his partnership,' the girls teased her. 'You are vicariously expressing your own inner rebel,' Sonia said primly.

She couldn't get enough of him. They had their own little project—the travel show.

One day, he told her he was taking her to the Yankee Stadium to watch baseball. But to her surprise, they never went inside; instead he took her to a hill and they watched the game from afar, under the stars, sucking on lollipops.

'And that's how you get the best view,' he said. 'Without even paying for it.' He kissed her. She kissed him back. *Oh my God*, she was falling more and more in love.

When the game let out, he put her on the
skateboard and ferried her down the hill
to interview all the crazy Yankee fans.
It was a thrill. He was thrilling to
be around.

When he was with her,
he was completely focused on
her but sometimes he would
disappear for a couple of days
and suddenly reappear with a
bunch of wild flowers.

She couldn't even be upset at
him. He was doing 'his thing', she
guessed, trying not to think too
much about what that was.

They were two people,
completely smitten with one another.
He carried her on his back all over New York if she so
much as said her feet hurt. He'd make her breakfast
before her eyes opened. He didn't have much money, but
he always brought her little thoughtful, imaginative gifts.
He made her feel like she was the most beautiful girl in
the world, and she was happy.

One day he got a pair of roller blades and presented
them to her with a warning, 'Careful, they are fast.' She
was excited and told Sonia she was going to Central Park
to ride them. Sonia broke down and begged her not to.
Sonia's cousin had had a fatal accident. She had fallen,
hit her head and died trying to roller blade. That was the
end of her roller blading dream.

She missed him. It had been five days; he had disappeared again. She dialled his number.

A woman's voice answered his mobile phone, and informed her he wasn't home. The woman said she was worried about him too. She asked the woman who she was. 'I'm his girlfriend. Who's this?'

She was shaking. Her world came crashing down yet again, just like the Twin Towers. She hung up and burst into tears. *GIRLFRIEND?*

Three days later, she met him at Strawberry Fields for the shoot they had planned earlier. Strawberry Fields is an area of Central Park that pays tribute to the singer, songwriter, musician and peace activist John Lennon.

She stood there in the crowd, her eyes tearing up. Crying was normal in the months after 9/11. An old man hugged her, tears pouring out of his eyes too.

Roller Boy came up from behind the trees on his skateboard. She looked at him accusingly.

He held her hand. With a frustratingly casual attitude he told her, 'You just showed up in my life and you're going back to India soon.'

'So?' she said, tears pouring out of her eyes.

'I had a girlfriend; what was I to do? Just drop her?'

She was going back to India, but the rest of his explanation made no sense.

'I don't want to see you again. Anyway, today is the last day for our shoot.'

She was hoping he'd say, 'No stay. Don't go, she is not my girlfriend, she is my sister. She was joking,' but he said nothing.

They shot at Strawberry Fields and the Dakota Apartments and then she walked away. She put on a brave face and her smile as they shot. And then, she went her way, and he went his.

She stopped seeing him completely after that. Every street in New York held memories of him. They'd jumped off the skateboard by that building; he'd carried her on his back on that street corner.

His smell, his crooked smile, his hair . . . she missed it all. She walked around New York in a daze, missing a certain Roller Boy, sucking on lollipops.

Two depressing months later, she was packing, ready to leave for India. She was on her last 100 dollars. But she had her show. She knew it would get picked up and soon she would be going around the world shooting. She started sobbing. Her dreams of Roller Boy and she travelling the world, shooting, had come tumbling down like Humpty Dumpty.

She called him. She *had* to see him one last time.

He rang the bell with a solemn look, his skateboard tucked under his arm. She opened the door and let him in.

He had a tape under his arm. A video tape. 'This was the day of 9/11. I went inside the towers on my skates when everyone was running outside and shot it. I want to give it to you,' he said.

An interesting parting gift. She accepted it.

He silently helped her with last-minute packing. They both shed a tear as they packed the tape of their show in her bag, right next to the 9/11 tape.

He then carried her bags down and dropped her to a cab. They looked into each other's eyes for the last time, both very teary.

'I am sorry,' he mumbled. 'You're special. I fell in love with you but you were always going back to India.'

'So, you kept your girlfriend on the side,' she said.

'I don't like being alone,' he said.

He kissed her. She kissed him back.

The Indian cab driver gave her a disapproving look.

They held hands, unaware. They both knew that this was something they had to let go of.

The cab driver impatiently honked. She reluctantly tore her hand and gaze away and sat in the cab.

She turned to look at him again. The car had started moving.

He immediately held on to the bumper of the cab and skated alongside. She was worried because this was dangerous, but she couldn't deny how sexy this felt, him skating besides her cab.

They went over the Brooklyn Bridge; he stayed there holding on to the cab looking at her, their eyes locked.

This was so risky; he could've been hurt but nothing had ever felt so romantic.

Once the cab got off the bridge, he turned and skated the other away. No words were spoken, just eyes, tears and skates.

That's how he was, that's how she will always remember him—on skates, his beautiful afro curls flying in the wind as he held on to her cab.

RECIPE

Puerto Rican-Mofongo

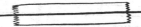

LESSON LEARNT

1. The same testosterone that makes bad boys sexy, bold, adventurous and rebellious also makes them less likely to follow the rules of dating and relationships.

2. Exciting and forbidden do not rhyme with stability and relationship.

3. Love stories do not have to be three-hour-long epic films, they can be short stories.

4. Bad boys are like a big chocolate cake that you can't stop eating. Indulging in them can leave you with a sugar rush that quickly turns into a stomach ache.

WHERE IS HE NOW?

Her suitcase got lost on the way back to India. Besides her clothes and cameras, she also lost all the footage that they had shot together. So, on arriving in India there was no show for the TV channels. She also never got to watch the tape that Roller Boy had recorded from 9/11. They lost touch.

THREE THANK YOU'S AND A SORRY:

1. She thanks him for opening up a world she would never have seen if not for him. Underground skate parks, graffiti mafia, hip hop bars in Harlem.

2. She thanks him for bringing out her inner bad girl.

3. She thanks him for helping her shoot her first travel pilot.

She is sorry she didn't carry the tape of 9/11 in her hand baggage and lost it.

SHE MISSES:

1. His cute afro, the mole on the right side of his face.

2. The sexy drawl, his lingo, the way he spoke that she found so adorable. 'Girl, I was doin' my thing.'

3. The amused look on his face when he looked at her.

14

HOW DOES YOUR BIGGEST LOVE TURN INTO YOUR BIGGEST DISAPPOINTMENT?

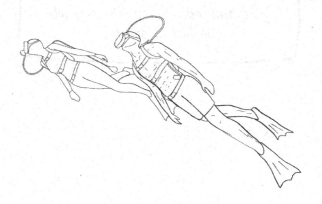

Quick update.

After moving back to India penniless and with no tape of the travel show, she had sworn off men.

She was going to fully focus on earning back all the money she had spent.

She moved back to her parents' house and didn't date anyone for a long time.

MTV refused to take her back because she had taken leave for three months and disappeared for six in New York.

She then met a director at a night club who asked her to audition for a movie.

She ended up acing the audition, and the movie turned out to be the biggest hit of the year, *Ishq Vishk*.

Her career was back on track. Money, not at all. Bollywood thinks they are doing you a favour when they cast you and don't pay you unless you're a star.

MTV invited her back as a host. Steady income was what she needed. So she rejected other Bollywood offers and chose the steady income, much to her co-stars' surprise.

She had briefly got back again with Frankenstein who took her to his friend's wedding in Phuket but she broke up with him when he threw his phone in the pool.

'I just asked him who he was texting and then I heard a splash. Who throws their own phone in the pool?' she said to the new girlfriends she had made in Phuket.

'Forget about him,' said Varsha. 'Come to my wedding! In Bangkok in June. And don't bring Frankenstein.'

And so, she flew to Bangkok in June, 2003.

It was a big fat Punjabi wedding. The first night was a youngsters' party. She was digging into a papaya salad when her new Bangkok friends, Shalini and Anuja, appeared.

'We want you to meet someone. He was in school with us, you may like him.'

She allowed herself to be pulled towards the door. Two tall guys were talking animatedly.

She was drawn to him at first sight.

He had big brown eyes, dark hair, dark eyebrows, a strong jawline; he was very engaged in telling a story. She doesn't remember the story, but she remembers the look on his face, the twinkle in his eye, his excitement while telling his funny story. He had none of the bad boy energy. In fact he seemed a bit nerdy.

She remembered Ruvani's words, 'We want the bad boy sperm—but not for marriage.'

This is the face of the man I would like to marry, she thought. *Wow, thank you, Shalini and Anuja!*

She joined the group, he looked at her shyly, she batted her eyelashes at him unconsciously and flicked her hair back.

'I like your camera,' he said, looking impressed with her Nikon with the long lens.

'Yes, I love shooting,' she said.

'Me too,' he said shyly.

They left the group and veered off on their own. He leaned against the piano.

'Your eyes are like big melting pools of coffee,' he said to her. She smiled shyly.

'I can't place your accent. Where are you from?' she asked softly. He told her he was Israeli but had grown up in Thailand and attended college in America—the University of Southern California (USC) film school on full scholarship. Just what she always wanted—creative, smart, funny. His good looks were a bonus.

'What do you do?' he asked.

'I work for MTV India as a veejay.'

'NO way,' he said. 'I direct and write a show for MTV Asia based out of Hong Kong.'

She laughed. 'You're kidding.'

'I am not,' he said.

It's meant to be, she thought in her head.

The piano against which he was leaning had a glass on it. The glass fell and he tried his best to catch it. It shattered. She noticed that his fingers were bleeding. 'I'm bleeding for you,' he said shyly.

She blushed and hurried away to get ice for his fingers. His fingers were still bleeding profusely when she came back. She iced it, her hands shaking a little with the physical contact. He put his fingers in his mouth and sucked them.

'Maybe a kiss from you will help,' he said. She blushed and kissed his fingers.

The next day was the sangeet. The theme was Las Vegas. She was wearing a short red dress. She scanned the crowd, looking for him. He was in the corner with his tall, bald friend; they were laughing. He was in a white shirt and black pants. Nothing Las Vegas about him, thank God. She liked his very understated look. He didn't even seem to know how tall and handsome he was.

As soon as he saw her, his eyes lit up. They shyly gravitated towards each other. The music started playing; they moved together to the music, smiling. They liked each other. It was sweet.

It was her birthday the next day, and he told her he had already made a plan for her. 'Meet me at the Shangri-La Hotel at 10 a.m.'

And so the next day, she met him with her Nikon and long lens in the lobby of the hotel, which was on the

Chao Phraya river. He had his Canon too. He led her outside, where he had booked a small two-seater boat.

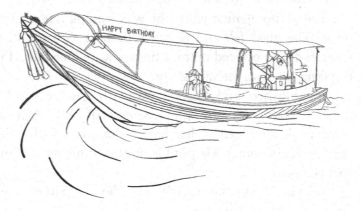

The motor was too loud and the boat smelled a little fishy, but for her it was so romantic. It made her feel as if she was in a Bollywood movie. She splashed her face with the river water. He smiled at her, a sweet, loving smile. His smile could light up a room. *Oh yes*, she thought to herself. *This is the face of the man I want to marry*.

They shot pictures of the kids jumping in the river, pointing out different things to each other. *This is so unexpected and romantic and what a lovely birthday, thank you God*, she thought. She splashed more water on her face and smiled as her eye caught his.

At the end of the trip, as they got out of the boat, he informed her that the river water was actually sewage. She was mortified.

He didn't have the heart to tell her this 'because you were having too much fun,' he said.

And so, a romance began.

They took motorbike taxis, he, she and the motor bike guy. All three of them on one bike! That's when he kissed her for the first time.

After her friend's wedding she said she was going to Koh Samui to get a license to dive by herself. He offered to accompany her. She accepted.

They stayed up all night, talking and laughing in Koh Samui. He seemed to know facts and trivia about everything, he was so interesting.

Yes, of course, she loved his beautiful smile and he was tall, broad shouldered and very good looking, but his brain was the most fascinating. The way he looked at the world intrigued her, and she could just listen to him talk all night. She had never met a guy this interesting.

He seemed calm from the outside but his nails were all bitten up. She asked him about it. He admitted he was very anxious inside. She saw none of that anxiety though. To her, he seemed just so serene or maybe that was just the stuff he was smoking.

That was Humble. She called him Humble because he was anything but pompous or conceited or grandiose and that was what she fell in love with.

He was not that selfie taking dude. Nor was he into what he wore. He was completely unaware of himself and a little shy. He was exactly the opposite of Roller Boy or even Frankenstein and the alpha male type.

He was prone to overthinking and he *convinced her* that scuba diving would lead to nitrogen build up in her brain.

And so, she ended up not getting her license on that trip even though that was what she had gone there for. She enjoyed just chilling with him—riding scooters around the island and taking long walks on the beach, swimming in the ocean, although he didn't want to go too deep like she did. He was not like the usual guy she met who just wanted to sleep with her; this guy was in sync with her brain. She did notice that he didn't try to have sex with her, and she wondered a little about it but then dismissed the thought.

They teased each other, saying it was a holiday romance. After all, he lived in Hong Kong and she in Mumbai.

On the day before she left for India, on the bus to the airport, he took his earphones out and put one ear piece in her ear and one in his and made her listen to the song 'Leaving on a jet plane'. That was the first time she heard the song. She wondered if the song was for her or that it just happened to play at the time. They held hands.

They returned to their homes.

But he'd call her every day with those little scratch cards from Hong Kong. This was pre-WhatsApp. He spent a lot of money and time to be in touch and she really appreciated it.

He made a proposition. He would get her on his show as a host and her fee would be monthly tickets to Hong Kong. That way, they could see each other every month.

Soon she was visiting Hong Kong at the end of every month. He'd always welcome her at the airport with a bunch of flowers, and they'd stay up all night talking and laughing, writing and shooting the show together.

She was in a relationship with this man, and it was wonderful. She had never met anybody like him—the way he looked at the world, a little obtuse and out of the box.

And he could always make her feel better.

If she was sad about something or even PMSing, he had a way of making her see the brighter side.

'He is loyal, honest and truthful,' she would tell her friends. 'I can leave him in a room full of naked women and he will do nothing.'

To which they would say, 'You can't trust any man blindly like that.' But she did. She believed she could trust Humble. After all he didn't even try to have sex with her. She thought about it for a few minutes and then dismissed it again.

Her boss at MTV India, Mr Chintamanu, who had a crush on her for years was not happy with this new romance. 'I am not giving you permission to go,' he'd say.

'But I shoot all my shows, finish all my responsibilities and then go,' she would argue.

'You still need to be around.'

'But why? Anyway, I don't shoot every day. I'm just going for one week every month. And it's also MTV.'

'MTV Asia and MTV India are different,' he replied.

'My show is still at Number 1. It's all going so well. So what's the problem if I go for one week every month to see my boyfriend?'

But Mr Chintamanu complained to Mr Boman Oshidaar that she was never available.

And one Tuesday afternoon they called her in to fire her.

'But my show is doing so well,' she said, shocked.

'Doesn't matter,' Mr Oshidaar said as he stared at her boobs. 'Have they grown?' he asked inappropriately. 'Anyway, nice boobs or not, you are fired.'

'I hate doing this,' said Mr Chintamanu, a tad too insincerely. 'I mean, I hope you're going to marry this guy that you're losing your job over.'

'But why?' she pleaded.

Mr Oshidaar continued, 'We are replacing you with VJ Anusa who is dying to do your show. Her boobs are like mosquito bites but she's hungry for work and you are distracted.'

'But I even gave up Bollywood movies so I could have this steady job.'

'Sorry! Our decision is final,' he said.

A tear ran down her face.

'And you look like a zebra,' Mr Oshidaar stated, 'Fair skin, black hair.' She didn't even know how to reply to that.

'And you still have the MTV Asia show with your boyfriend,' Mr Chintamanu stated.

'They don't pay me,' she mumbled. 'I do it for the free tickets.'

She put her sunglasses on, held her head high as tears poured down her face and walked out of the office. VJ Anusa, sitting on the bench outside, looked very excited.

She walked out of the office, her heart in her hands, crying. This felt like the biggest break-up she had had. She had worked with them on and off for ten years. It had lasted longer than every boyfriend. How could they end it like that? It was so unfair.

She was heartbroken. And depressed. She couldn't even look at the TV any more.

But Humble was there for her, soothing her on the phone, making her see this as an opportunity and not as a failure. He was the best. 'Can you have the perfect boyfriend and the perfect career?' she wondered. Maybe you just get one at a time.

She decided to fly to Hong Kong and live with him full time.

He encouraged her to write. He introduced her to watch films she hadn't heard of. He made her watch foreign films, German films, Persian films, French films.

They discussed film making. She watched him edit.

He was her creative mentor and partner. He was the film school she had always wanted to go to.

They, according to her, were the perfect little team, always setting off on a little project together, travelling, taking pictures, writing stories, making short films.

They had so much to talk about, they made each other laugh, they stayed up all night talking, they even had their own code language. *This relationship is perfect! We are so compatible.*

The only thing they lacked was money. His show also got cancelled and they were both jobless.

But they weren't big spenders. They lived on a budget and managed. But sometimes, she felt a little ball of sadness in the pit of her belly. She tried to push it away, but it kept coming back. It wasn't that they had no money or that they were always counting pennies and budgeting.

It was that they were talking, *just* talking into the night.

There was not a lot of physical stuff going on. He didn't seem to want to be physically intimate. If they did it, she would initiate it. And most times he would reject the idea.

But we have so much fun together. We have each other's backs. It was him and me against the world. Isn't that what love is? Shouldn't this be enough for me?

She didn't want to leave him. Was she going to leave him because of a lack of physical intimacy?

What's more important, compatibility or sex?

He was family. They lived together too. They had a home together.

They moved from Hong Kong to Bangkok because Bangkok was much cheaper.

She got some calls to act in Bollywood films but she was now working with him to make another pilot for a travel show. Her second attempt with a different boyfriend! The lack of physical intimacy was the only teeny-weeny issue they had. She tried to talk to him about this 'small' problem. 'Could we perhaps try to turn on some heat, be more like lovers than friends who love each other?' He told her he didn't think they had a problem and if she wanted 'heat', she should just get it elsewhere or take a cold shower. That was the first time he was nasty to her. She scribbled in her diary, 'Mismatched libidos, it's like trying to enjoy a fine dining experience with someone who has a completely different appetite. It's like ordering a spicy curry dish when your partner prefers a plain salad.'

She wondered, *Will we find a harmonious blend that satisfies both our appetites?*

They started arguing about this issue. He started getting angry, defensive, throwing stuff.

He started picking on her.

Her brain, her hair, her clothes: he started criticizing all of it. His endearing humour turned into hurtful sarcasm.

Her beautiful prince turned into a frog.

Maybe he's just not attracted to me in that way. Maybe I'm not attractive in that way any more. Is it me? Maybe I am too fat or perhaps my ass is not big enough. Self-doubt about her appearance crept in.

But when she was on her period or if they didn't talk about their lack of sexual intimacy, they laughed and enjoyed each other's thoughts and energy.

If she suggested leaving, his eyes would tear up. *He did love her.* They had an emotional and a mental connection. *Isn't this enough? Who gets everything?* She would talk herself into accepting it. But it grew harder and harder for her.

She felt she was pushing her sexuality away, repressing what made her a woman. And she started resenting him for that.

He wanted to cuddle but she started hating his cuddles. She needed more than hugs and kisses on her cheeks.

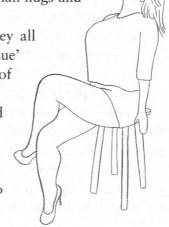

The fights started, and they all revolved around this 'little issue' that had grown into a ball of negativity between them.

She would leave him and tell him she was going for a walk. And when she would return, he would say, 'Back so soon?' As if he wanted her to stay away longer.

If she wore a short skirt, he would say, 'Put on some clothes. Cross your legs.'

If she wore a sexy nightie, he would laugh and say, 'You look funny.'

'You're always available,' he complained one day.

'But we live together,' she said. 'Do I need to play games to make this relationship work?'

He shrugged and went back to his laptop.

Was this what she had signed up for? She was now thirty years old!

Love without physical intimacy?

'Okay fine, if you want to, let's. But you do all the work. I've had a long day,' he would say.

He was frustrated with his work situation too; he was very talented but wasn't that good with people.

He wasn't getting any jobs and they were tight on money. She tried to console him and see the bigger picture—they were going to make a travel show together. But he snapped at her, 'This travel show is your dream. It's not my dream. I want to make movies.'

'And you will,' she said. 'Just one step at a time.'

He looked at her coldly and said, 'What do you know, you are just an effing veejay.'

Tears ran down her cheeks as she ran to the other room to cry.

She had put in her own money to shoot another pilot for another travel show. But this time, he wasn't going on the shoot; she had hired a crew. He encouraged her and gave her his equipment to shoot.

The night before she was leaving for Malaysia to shoot, she brought up the 'little issue' again and he threw the tripod on the wall in anger. It just missed hitting her.

'Stop pressuring me,' he yelled. 'Go get it somewhere else.'

She went to sleep sobbing.

She got on the plane the next day with big bags under her eyes. *What's happening to my perfect love? Is it not perfect after all? Maybe he was just frustrated with his career, maybe he has a physical deficiency or low testosterone or something. Or maybe it's me. Maybe I am unattractive.* She made up all kinds of excuses. She did not want to leave her prince. She fell asleep on the plane feeling very disturbed. When her eyes opened, she noticed that the videographer from her team was staring at her. He was covered in tattoos and had long hair tied in a ponytail. His upper body reminded her of Popeye. She looked away.

Later in the hotel, when she was discussing the shoot with him, he stared into her eyes for a little too long than what was considered appropriate. She wasn't sure if it made her uncomfortable or excited. He was giving her a lot of attention. She turned away.

They were shooting in the middle of the night in Malaysia at a crowded festival called Thaipusam. This was where people pierced their bodies and went into a trance from the pain and adrenaline. There was a lot of energy in the air. It was night but the whole city felt awake, pumping and alive, hearts beating, bodies sweating, people going into physical trance. She ran around with the cameraman, aka Popeye, taking shots. Later the team split ways to take separate shots.

It was still crowded at 4 a.m., and she couldn't find her team. She was lost. She looked around in the light of the full moon and walked among the millions of sweaty people.

Suddenly from the back, someone held her hand, firmly. She looked up, it was Popeye, staring into her eyes. She walked with him in the crowded streets, her body aware of his hand in hers. She felt a stab of guilt but did not pull away. *This shouldn't be happening.* She loved her boyfriend. But she was mad at him too; he never held her hand like this, this firm, this tight, this strong. He didn't look into her eyes like this.

She felt like a woman again.

And so a guilty 'hand-holding' romance started between Popeye and her in the jungles of Malaysia. They didn't have much to talk about. It was a lot of staring in the eyes and tight hand holding when nobody was looking. At the end of the trip, she told Popeye she was going to break up with Humble.

Popeye started at her with his piercing eyes. 'I don't do relationships. I'm going back to my life.'

'But don't you ever want to have a companion? What about kids?' she asked him.

'Look at the traffic! I can't believe people still have kids,' he said.

She nodded. He did have a point.

So she went back home to Bangkok with a hole in her heart and tried to keep making it work with Humble. But she couldn't stop dreaming of the tight hand holding and piercing brown eyes. As she lay awake at night she thought, 'A relationship without sex? Or sex without a relationship? What is better?'

No, Humble was not gay. This thought had crossed her mind too, but his sexual identity wasn't the issue here.

When she heard her girlfriends complain about oversexed boyfriends or husbands, she'd feel a pang of jealousy.

Humble was always 'too full, too hungry, too tired, not in the mood'.

She did research. She asked almost every woman she met and discovered that one of the world's biggest myths was that men wanted it all the time and women were the ones with the excuses.

When she kissed him, she felt him pushing her away with one arm and pulling her close with the other. She pointed this out to him. He had tears in his eyes, he was struggling too.

Then it started getting weirder. He started speaking to her in a baby voice and got very upset if she dressed up or wore make-up.

She stopped dressing up. She dressed down. She just wanted to please him. They had moved back to India, she was all dressed up or dressed down (as he liked it). 'Date night finally, after so long,' she said to him smiling.

'Oh,' he said, 'Cyril just called; it's boys night.'

'But but we had a plan?'

'It's boys night, babe.'

'Okay,' she said, 'I will stay home.' She took her shoes off as he walked out of the door.

'It's good you're making friends in India,' she said. The door banged shut.

Two hours later she texted Cyril who was her friend but had become his friend. 'How's boys night?' she asked.

Cyril replied, 'Why are you not here? All the girls are here too.'

'Oh,' she said, 'does Humble know?'

'Of course,' Cyril replied, 'he's here with us.' He sent her a picture of Humble at the table, which had more girls than boys.

She was hurt. What was happening? Why didn't he want her around.

'You're always around,' he announced when he came home a little tipsy. 'Sometimes I want to go out without you.'

She gave it a lot of thought. She spent many a night awake, wondering why this was happening. Soon, she hardly slept at all. She developed insomnia. She knew she loved him. But she didn't feel so loved anymore. She scribbled in her notes, 'In a relationship, do both partners ever love each other equally? Or is it normal for one to be more into the other?'

She stayed with Humble for many years. Their love story spanned across many countries and continents. She'd run into Popeye, and they'd engage in some eye flirting and hand-holding. But Popeye was very clear that he wanted nothing more than that.

When she would mention a relationship, he'd say, 'I can barely look after my plants; my plants are dying.'

If she refused to hold his hand, he'd say, 'Flow flow, you're not flowing, you have stopped flowing.'

She went to the same yoga class as Popeye and watched him leave with different women. It would sting but she had Humble, who was always there for her with his sparkling brown eyes and bright smile, funny stories, engaging, fascinating ideas and thoughts.

She thought maybe if he worked out, he'd build more testosterone and then perhaps he would want to be physical. She asked him to join her in the gym. 'The only part of my body I am working out is my brain,' he replied and that was the end of that conversation.

Life is ironic. Humble didn't want anything physical. Popeye didn't want anything emotional. If only they were both one person.

Was it some sort of cosmic mistake or was that just how real life was? *Have the rom-coms been lying to us all this while? Am I settling by choosing a stable relationship over passion? But really how stable is this relationship?*

One day, as she and Humble stood waiting for the subway in New York (which was where they had moved to at the time because she had got a role on a big show on ABC Network there. He had moved with her.) He turned towards her and said, 'I want to be with an ugly woman now. I have had too much of pretty.'

Two days later on the phone he told her that he wanted to be with a Jewish woman, someone from his culture. 'India was an experience, now I want to go back home,' he said.

She felt like he was telling her she was a country that was fun to visit but not to stay in, not to settle down.

He decided to move out overnight. 'We need to stop speaking for some time,' he declared.

She tried calling him. Then she tried again. And again. No reply.

After fifteen missed calls, he texted, 'Don't call me. I am with a Jewish woman now, someone from my culture, and she doesn't appreciate it.'

That was it. That was the end?

She wrote him long paragraphs but got no reply. Until, one day, he finally blocked her.

She walked around New York with tears in her eyes. Life had never felt lonelier.

Humble taught her many things. One of them was to appreciate a good salad.

Even today, many years later, when she finds herself missing Humble, she makes the Israeli salad that he taught her, sits down and thinks of his face when he would tell his funny stories. Nobody else completed her thoughts and her sentences, when she'd think of something or say something, the way Humble did.

Everybody has a great love. Humble was hers. Maybe not in the earth shattering, sensual way where she saw stars when they kissed. In fact they rarely kissed.

He didn't rock her world in the way most lovers rock each other's.

But she had loved him more than she had ever loved anyone. There was no doubt about that.

'You put me on a pedestal' was one of the last things he had said to her which had made her wonder.

'Are we more attracted to the idea of someone rather than the reality?'

She had been so sure that he was 'the one'. But can you ever truly know if someone is 'the one'.

Does 'the one' stay 'the one' forever?

Is there just one 'one'? Or are there many 'ones'?

RECIPE

Israeli salad and a river of tears

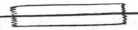

LESSON LEARNT

1. She learnt that every relationship needs a balance of mental, physical and emotional connection, and it's impossible to have all three in equal proportions.

2. She learnt that people can leave a relationship without physically leaving the relationship by just ignoring your needs and treating you poorly.

3. She learnt people can betray you not just by cheating but by withholding.

4. She learnt there are no fairy tale endings and 'the one' is most likely just an illusion.

5. She learnt you have to know it's time to leave the relationship if you feel that you have to apologize for who you are.

6. She discovered mismatched libidos are like serving a sparkling champagne to someone who prefers a soothing cup of herbal tea. It's a clash of intensities that can leave both parties feeling unsatisfied, lonely and out of sync.

15

Is it Wiser to Follow Your Head or Your Heart or Your Hormones?

Summer of 2011
New York City

She sent Humble yet another text. 'I miss you.' No reply. Her inner monologue was like, 'I told you so, bro.'

Quick update:

She had lost her job; the ABC Network show that she had been working on for two years had got cancelled. The film she had acted in, *Delhi Belly*, was a massive hit in India. But the pay cheque? Rs 2 lakh, which evaporated quicker than ice cream on a hot day in New York. Whoever believed actors were rolling in dough? Well, this is a scoop of the reality of being an actor. She had to downgrade her apartment.

She was staying in New York just to be in the same city as him. He now had a job here and she didn't. She knew if she went back to India, she would never see him again.

She was walking the streets aimlessly, tears in her eyes, head in the clouds, not even looking up while crossing the street. Through her tears, she spotted someone gliding towards her. That half smile, mole on the face, short afro, the familiar glide.

Oh my God, it was Roller Boy! Nine years later!

She hadn't thought she would see him again. But there he was.

He stopped.

Their eyes locked and they gave each other a tight hug. He lifted her up, both so happy to meet after all those years. She felt an electric current run through her entire body.

He looked different, he dressed different, his afro was almost gone. How many years had it been? It looked like a steam roller had gone over him. He had aged, not well, but he had the same effect on her.

She and Roller Boy were swept into a whirlwind romantic affair; it felt like they were back in 2001.

This was her second journey with Roller Boy nine years later!

They were attracted to each other, they were passionate.

He filled all the gaps Humble had left.

Roller Boy felt it was meant to be, meeting again like that after nine years! He was all in. No girlfriend on the side this time, he assured her. He was just so in love with her.

But sometimes, when she woke up in the brownstone of Roller Boy's Harlem apartment, she stared at the bookcase in front of the bed. It was filled with shoes. Sneakers.

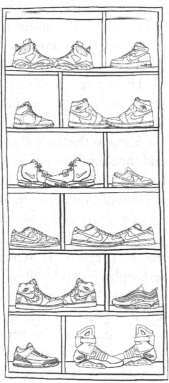

Humble had a bookshelf full of books and Roller Boy had a bookcase full of shoes. And this was what she was trying to digest.

Roller Boy interrupted her introspection with a passionate kiss. Fifteen minutes later he came back with breakfast on a tray. He placed it on the bed and kissed her again. She smiled at him. *What's wrong with me? This is what I wanted. Why am I fighting it?*

Roller Boy left for work; he now had his own production company. He was struggling but at least he wasn't selling marijuana on the streets anymore like he did in 2001.

She was still a little wary of him and his love for women. He still flirted with waitresses when they went out for dinner, and she often caught his eye wandering. She comforted herself with the thought that he was madly in love *with her* and tried to ignore everything else.

Her patience lasted till the day he disappeared for an hour with some Scandinavian woman he was working with and left her alone at the bar they had been at. His reply was, 'You're still not over Humble and I feel it.'

They argued. A lot. And didn't communicate well at all.

His energy level also was still the same, and she struggled to keep up with the all-night parties and then 7 a.m. wake-up calls.

She was thinking about the previous night's argument and the Scandinavian woman when she saw that Humble had emailed her out of the blue.

'Should we get back together? Should we try and move on to the next step? Have a baby? That's the best creation. We created screenplays and films and shows, let's create a baby. I still love you.'

She stared at the email, at a loss for words. She didn't know how to react.

The most difficult period of her life now began. One would think that being caught between two men whom you love is a very romantic and beautiful thing but there can be nothing worse.

On the one hand, she finally had the passion, sensuality and chemistry that she'd been craving. On the other, she had stability, reliability, safety and a family calling.

Plus, for the first time in years, Humble had a good job.

Roller Boy already had his family. He had a son and a baby mama. She had never met her. That too was a source of argument that had taken place when she had found out she wasn't invited to his son's birthday. He spent the weekends with them and kept her separate. She felt very alone when he went away to his 'family'.

She stared at the computer screen and the glaring question about the baby. 'Let me think about this.'

She hit send.

When Roller Boy came home that night, he told her he had some event he wanted to take her to. It was another long night of booze and partying and while it was sexy and fun, she was *tired* and thinking how long this would keep her happy. What was her future with Roller Boy?

And so the war began. The war between her head and her heart and her hormones.

She started making pro and con lists for both the men. She wrote incessantly in her journal. She was torn. She felt ripped in the middle. Soon she didn't recognize what her head was saying and what her heart was saying. She became distracted and forgetful. She just couldn't make a decision.

She started seeing Humble on the weekends for lunch while Roller Boy was with his baby mama and son. They laughed and told stories; it was like old times. Also, Humble was a creative director at NBC now. He could afford the restaurants that they both used to dream of but never enter.

'Thank you, for standing by me in my darkest times,' Humble said.

'I always knew you would make it,' she said.

The bill came; he insisted on paying.

'You were a good woman to me,' he said, 'always saving my money, paying for things when I had nothing. Please let me take care of the bill now.'

She allowed him.

Meanwhile Roller Boy was struggling, so when they went to dinners, she paid or they went to smaller hole-in-the-wall places like the ones she used to go to before, when Humble didn't have work. She was also struggling with money. New York was expensive and even though she was getting small roles here and there it didn't allow her any luxuries.

Roller Boy was very possessive and territorial. Guess that comes with passion. He wasn't happy with her lunches with Humble. They argued about how he had different rules for himself and for her.

But the way he looked at her, like in the movies, his eyes shone with passion and he couldn't keep his hands off her. It felt so good to be desired like that. She scribbled in her notes, 'Is there ever a balance between our need for stability and our need for adventure in a relationship? Could both possibly come from one person?'

She had to fly back to India to shoot a film. She and Roller Boy were away from each other for a month. She missed him.

'I'm coming to India,' he declared on a video call one day. 'I have bought my ticket.'

'Oh my God, isn't it too expensive for you?' she asked.

'I don't care,' he said. 'I can't be without you.'

She was excited he was coming to India to see her.

The shoot was in Sula Vineyard. He arrived at 1 a.m. They were all over each other, so excited to be together after a month.

The next morning he accompanied her to the set. He sat next to her, holding her hand.

When she had to go for a shot, she gave him her laptop for safekeeping.

As she said her lines, she had a horrible feeling as she saw Roller Boy go through her computer. She was shooting for half an hour. He was just staring at the screen.

The scene ended. She ran up to him. He put the laptop under his arm and walked away with tears in his eyes. She ran after him.

'I am going to the hotel room.' He walked a few steps. Stopped. Turned around to face her. 'And I would have had a family with you if you wanted.'

She felt her heart sinking in her chest. He had read Humble's email about having a baby.

She begged him to stay. He walked off with the laptop. She had to stay for the next six hours and shoot. She was in a daze. Her character had to be funny and happy. This was so challenging that day as her heart was sinking slowly.

When she finally made her way back to the hotel room, he was packing up and getting ready to leave.

'But you came all the way from New York. This is your first night here, please please don't leave,' she begged and pleaded.

'I know everything,' he said. 'Everything. Everything.'

'Your pros and cons list. Your emails to your friends debating if you should leave me. My bookshelf full of sneakers and his bookshelf full of books. I've read your journal. I know *everything*.'

He left the room. She chased him. He ran through the vineyards. She ran after him. It was like a bad scene from a Bollywood film. But there was no stopping him. He was gone.

The next seven days were unpleasant, to say the least. She had booked a hotel for them in Juhu. She ended up sleeping on the king-sized bed alone. She was still shooting and he was nowhere to be found. She tried his number all the time; it was turned off. She knew he was still in India, but he wasn't responding to her at all.

On the night before his flight he finally came to the hotel to see her. He silently hugged her.

Both were sobbing. Humans are flawed.

Why do we only realize a good thing when its leaving?

Where had he been all these days? 'Colaba,' he said, not getting into much detail.

After that, everything changed between Roller Boy and her.

He didn't break up with her, but he turned cold and mean. And she took it because she felt she deserved it.

He was too hurt and too angry, and he just couldn't get over it. But he still didn't let her go. He would disappear for weeks and then come back with tears in his eyes. *I miss your smell, I miss your taste, I miss you!* And she would take him back because she felt this was all her fault.

She couldn't afford an apartment anymore, she declared to him.

'I have to move back to India.'

'Move in with me,' said Roller Boy.

And so she did. It was a brownstone in Harlem. But he would disappear for weeks from the house, leaving her alone with his room-mate, an older African American woman, who had a heart of gold but a terrible drinking and drug problem. She got very sick while he was away—she was bleeding and it wasn't stopping. She needed a doctor. But she had no insurance. It was America; doctors were expensive.

She looked up the Internet, and found a Russian doctor who seemed reasonably priced and had good reviews.

The Russian doctor examined her, took some blood tests and then very calmly told her, 'You have cancer!'

What?

Her whole life flashed before her eyes.

Was she going to die here in New York alone and lonely?

She walked around New York for three days not telling anyone.

After three days, she called Humble. He immediately took her to another doctor and waited patiently in the waiting room. She came out smiling. She did not have cancer after all. It was just an egg that had burst. She was so relieved. So was he. They hugged crying!

She went back to Roller Boy's home. He was still away.

It was 22 October 2012. The day Hurricane Sandy hit and New York lost power. It was dark and cold. She and Roller Boy had yet another big argument. He was yelling at her.

No heat, no light. She was freezing in his Harlem apartment.

It was minus 5 degrees. Imagine sleeping with jackets and socks and shoes on and still shivering.

She was in the darkest and most confused place she had ever been in.

She decided to leave Roller Boy's house and go back to Humble.

So she packed a small bag and left Harlem in the middle of a cold autumn night.

As she got out of the subway, she just sat on the side of the road with all her bags. Was she doing the right thing?

Humble was overjoyed to see her. He apologized for cutting her off.

Hurricane Sandy was looming over the city. They bought candles and blankets and food and went back to his place in China Town. They talked and laughed, and it felt comfortable and secure. But her heart was torn.

People ask you, are you listening to your head or your heart? But she didn't know which one was saying what at that point. Her heart and head were a jumbled mess.

If ever there was a romantic time to be together, it was Hurricane Sandy. All huddled up in candlelight, no power to charge phones. If they were ever going to be romantic, it was going to be now.

But *nothing* romantic happened. They were like old friends, a brother and sister who loved one another dearly.

Is that what relationships become over time? Can you love someone and desire them at the same time? Why does good intimacy not guarantee good sex or in her case any sex at all? Why does compatibility not lead to sex?

The power came back. Hurricane Sandy had ended. They hadn't even kissed. She tried her best to forget Roller Boy's kisses. Or not wonder what he was doing. Who he was kissing. Surely he was mad at her and not going to wait. She cried in the bathroom. *Why am I here?*

She ached to call Roller Boy but what would she even say? She had walked away, abandoned him in the middle of a cold autumn night, leaving nothing behind but her fluffy slippers.

Humble knocked on the bathroom door. They were in the middle of a Woody Allen movie marathon. Next up was the film *Husbands and Wives*. They lay on the bed and marvelled at Woody Allen's script, chatting like old friends, so much love for each other but still no chemistry, no spark. She felt hollow.

The next day they binge watched *Homeland*. A sex scene came on. As she watched the characters passionately look into each other's eyes, she started sobbing. He looked at her in pain.

In that moment, she turned to Humble and told him they needed to end it. He hadn't even touched her, she said.

He didn't want her to go, he loved her. So, he tried. They tried. It was awkward.

They couldn't do it. It felt so forced.

They both ended up at the edge of the bed crying. It was over. They both knew it. How could they have a baby without even having sex? Without being able to even kiss? They sobbed hugging each other, but it was time to say goodbye forever.

They promised they would always be friends. Always have each other's back.

A day later, with tears in her eyes, she bought a one-way ticket to Tulum, Mexico, and left New York City.

She was done with both of them. She had lost herself.

I need to be with me. Just me.

I need to make ME my partner.

After all, I am my longest commitment.

She got on the plane to Mexico and let out a deep breath. She should have done this a long time ago. Half crying, half smiling, she showed her boarding pass to the air hostess.

RECIPE
Khichdi?

LESSON LEARNT

1. She learnt that emotional connection does not guarantee good sex.

2. A hot passionate romance does not guarantee compatibility.

3. People come into our life for a season, a reason or a lifetime. When we put them in the wrong category, that's when we hurt most.

4. Forcing sexual chemistry is like trying to create a fusion dish with mismatched ingredients that simply don't work together.

WHERE IS HE NOW?

Humble is a distant memory now. He lives in a fancy apartment in Tribeca, New York, with his wife and two kids.
He is the creative director of NBC.

They are not friends.

THREE THANK YOU'S AND A SORRY:

1. She thanks him for being her best friend, her confidant, her film school and her travel partner for so many years.

2. She thanks him for inspiring her to write scripts and edit videos.

3. She thanks him for showing her that she was more than just a pretty face and that she can be more than just an actor or a veejay.

She is sorry she stayed with him for years when he gave her all the signs that he was just not that into her.

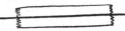

SHE MISSES:

1. The way he looks at the world. A little off-centre.

2. His sense of humour— dark but so funny.

3. Him as a creative partner and friend, discussing ideas and stories and scripts.

16

WHEN IT COMES TO MATTERS OF THE HEART, DOES ANYBODY HIT THE JACKPOT?

As she wandered around Tulum, Mexico, by herself, there were times she felt free and times she felt lonely. The beginning had been hard but she had been doing yoga every day, swimming in the ocean, eating good food. She was healing.

31 December 2013. On the last day of the year, she wanted to go for a swim. There was an old man sitting on the beach. He looked quite trustworthy. 'Can I leave my purse here, while I go swim?' she asked. 'Of course, I will watch it,' he said smiling.

She came out of the ocean two hours later with her swimming cap and googles on, looking for the old man. There he was, but, wait, next to him was a very handsome tall gentleman. Muscular, shirtless, tanned, with blue eyes, blonde flowing hair, sipping orange juice. The old man pointed at her. The young man jumped up. 'Oh there you are,' he said. 'My father said we should wait for you; come join us for lunch. We have ordered some fish tacos.'

She was speechless. God, I wish I looked better, she thought. She pulled off her swimming cap and googles. 'Sure,' she said, trying not to look at his rippling arms and six-pack abs.

And so they had lunch on the beach. The tacos were delicious. Blue-eyed, ripped man had a sense of humour and a British accent. His dad was funny too. 'So what's your plan this evening?' he asked. She stared at him blankly. 'Don't tell me you have no plan, it is New Year's eve.' She shook her head, feeling like an idiot. 'No plan,' she replied. 'You see, I am travelling alone. You're the first people I am having a real conversation with in fifteen days,' she said laughing.

'Dad, can I invite her?' he asked his dad in his crisp British accent. 'Of course,' his dad replied in his German accent. 'You must join us tonight. We are going to the "Be Tulum" House Party.'

'Wait,' she replied, 'that's 300 dollars per person. I can't go,' she laughed.

'No way,' Blue Eyes said, 'I have an extra ticket which will go waste, please just come. I will be disappointed if you don't.'

'But . . .' she said.

'I insist,' he replied firmly.

She got lost for a second in his eyes. They were the colour of the ocean. *Oh man! What luck.*

'Okay,' she said, smiling.

'We will pick you up at 9 p.m.,' his dad said.

'Bye, bye,' he said and as she gave him her cheek to kiss, he missed and pecked her half on her cheek, half lips.

She blushed, feeling tingly all over.

'See you tonight,' he said and squeezed her hand.

And so, she went back to her hotel, singing. Mr Germany with the Brit accent was so attractive. She couldn't believe she actually had a date for New Year's eve. And what a nice guy, there with his dad, she thought.

That night, father and son picked her up. They sat in his open jeep, and she got swept off to the 'Be Tulum House Party'.

It was a stunning hotel. The whole place was lit like a fairytale. As she walked with him and his dad into the place, she felt a deep sense of gratitude. *See, the universe always has my back*, she said to herself smiling.

'This is our section,' Blue Eyes said, leading her to one side of the pool. There was a long table and at it there were about *thirteen other young women*. They were all gorgeous, impeccably dressed and rushed to meet Blue Eyes as soon as they entered. She stood to one side with his dad.

The girls were all over him. He sat at the head of the table, his dad sat at the other end. And the girls sat in between. *What is going on?*

Her date had turned into *an orgy*!

She scribbled on her phone, 'This feels like a luscious-looking cake that crumbled disappointingly before I even tasted it.'

She sat at the end of the table with his dad. *Oh well*, she thought. *It's better than being alone in my room.* And the girls were quite friendly.

'You are from India, how exotic. That's my spirit country!' a blonde busty girl exclaimed.

'What's your spirit country?' Busty Blonde asked her.

She thought about it. 'India too, I guess,' she mumbled.

'Let's go to the bathroom,' said the blonde.

'Oh okay,' she said and got up. Two other blonde girls with Kim Kardashian buttocks joined them. 'Isn't he so hot?' they all whispered to each other.

'What's the deal with him?' she asked them. 'All of you are so into him.'

'Don't you know?' one of the blonde Kim Kardashians replied. 'He's the youngest billionaire in Europe. He just

sold his company. A self-made billionaire. He's so cool.'
The girls giggled in awe.

'Oh', she said, disappointed. He was rich and good
looking.

Awful combination!

The universe is playing games with me.

They went back to the table. The music started and
everyone got up to dance. She sipped her wine. He looked
at her, winked and called her to join in as he danced with
three ladies. 'Come here, little Indian girl,' he said.

'Sorry, I am not joining your harem,' and with that
she got up and left the table.

Her phone beeped. It was Humble.

'Happy New Year. I've met a Jewish woman. She
doesn't want me to be in touch with you. I will be
blocking this number.'

She sat down on a rock. The music was blaring. A
tear trickled down her face.

Ten-nine-eight-seven . . . the countdown began.
'Happy New Year,' everyone yelled!

She texted Humble back: 'Happy New Year to you
too. Please don't block me, we promised we would
always be friends.'

She hit send. OMG, his profile pic had disappeared.
He had already blocked her! WHAT??

From Bae to Blocked, just like that?

'Happy New Year,' Busty Blonde screamed and came
up and kissed her on her lips. Ugh, this was not what she
had in mind when she came to this party.

'Let's dance, Indian girl,' she said. 'I want to learn
some Bollywood moves.'

She spent the night dancing with Busty Blonde and also trying to dodge her kisses. 'I don't swing that way,' she shouted over the music. 'Believe me, I wish I did!'

'Try it,' Busty Blonde urged her, 'you will never need a man again. I'm so good with my tongue and fingers.'

'NO NO, you're beautiful but really no! So sorry. I respect and appreciate the offer.'

The sun was rising; she walked back to her hotel by herself on the beach. It was a sunrise beach and as she saw the sun coming up, the orange ball out of the sea, and the crowd dancing with drums welcoming in the new year, she thought to herself about the past year.

What a confusing year!

She was doing better. Much better. She had found herself again. She breathed in the morning air and smiled. Hello Me! I'm finally all right again.

Her phone beeped. It was an unknown number. 'Stay away from Humble. He's mine.'

OMG. The Jewish woman was texting her. Why?

'We promised each other we would always be friends,' she texted her back.

'You're an unmarried, desperate, childless woman in your thirties. Stay the eff away from us.'

Her hands started trembling. Childless? Unmarried? Desperate?

Wow, this chick really knows how to throw insults and hit me where it hurts.

She tried to think of a smart comeback but all she could text back was, 'How old are you?'

Her phone beeped again.

'I'm twenty-nine. And by the way, I am pregnant with his child,' she wrote, 'and we are getting married in a few days.'

She choked and threw her phone in the sand.

RECIPE
Fish tacos

LESSON LEARNT

1. Men move on fast.

2. When things get overwhelming, buy a ticket and get the hell out of there!

3. And oh, some things, like blue eyes are just too good (looking) to be true.

4 Just as a dish may dazzle with its presentation, it's the taste and substance that truly matter.

5. I am my longest and most important commitment.

WHERE IS HE NOW?

She would like to look Blue Eyes up on Instagram and see; but she doesn't even remember his full name.

THREE THANK YOU'S AND A SORRY:

1. She thanks him for the most memorable New Year's eve of her life (even though it didn't go as she expected).

2. She thanks him for cheering her up in Tulum.

3. She thanks him for introducing her to Busty Blonde. We are still Facebook friends.

She is sorry for judging him about the harem.

17

CAN YOU MOVE ON TO A FUTURE WHEN YOUR PAST IS STILL PRESENT?

After Tulum, she decided to go to India for a bit to meet her parents. She missed home. The show that she had been doing in the US for two years had been unexpectedly cancelled. She had left both Humble and Roller Boy behind in New York.

She got an email, 'Do you like Pink Floyd?' It was from a producer whom she had seen giving a talk on stage. They had briefly been introduced for five minutes.

'Maybe there's a Pink Floyd concert and he wants me to host it,' she told her mom excitedly. She wrote back, 'Yes, I love Pink Floyd and Roger Waters and have followed his journey closely.' Then she started researching about Roger Waters. *What an opportunity this would be!* she thought. *But why is he asking me?*, she wondered. *Maybe he heard about my MTV background.*

She got another email. 'Want to go to the concert?'

'Do you want me to host it?' she asked.

'No no, I am just inviting you to the concert. It's in Paris. As a guest.' She was confused. *Why was he inviting her?*

'I am in India,' she replied.

'That's not a problem, I will send you a ticket.'

That night she spoke to her friends at Bombay Gym. 'Why is he inviting me?' she asked. This was before she was an 'influencer'.

'Maybe it's a date,' her friend Preeta replied.

'A date! In Paris. At a Pink Floyd concert?'

'Is he hot?' her friends asked.

'He is tall and seemed very cool. The gay guys were swooning over him. I don't remember his face.'

Oh my God, they were right, he was asking her on a date.

'Should I go?'

'Of course,' her friends screamed. Preeta googled him.

'OMG! You're going on a date with an American billionaire to Paris!'

She wrote back to him that night, 'Can I have my own room?'

'Of course,' he replied. 'I am not comfortable sharing rooms on the first date. And please, no expectations. Don't expect me to sleep with you, just because we are in Paris.'

She laughed. Okay, the pressure was off.

The next day, his assistant called her for details and booked her a first-class ticket to Paris! She was going on a date to the Pink Floyd concert.

She got there a day before him, well rested on first class. There was a black chauffeur-driven limo waiting for her at the airport. She got in and got dropped off at the Mandarin Oriental.

She opened the door to her room. It wasn't just a hotel room, it was a suite, and it was filled with beautiful flowers. There was a note that read: 'Sorry I am not there before you but enjoy your time in Paris.'

Oh my God, was he kidding? She felt like she was in a *Sex in the City* episode in Paris. She got dressed up feeling like Emily in Paris before the show was even made. Then she went sight-seeing with the chauffeur. 'Lenny Kravitz really likes this café,' he said when she said she wanted to get some coffee. 'He was sitting right where you are two days ago.'

'Oh,' she said eyeing the chauffeur. He was quite hot with his cute accent but she needed to focus on her date tomorrow.

She was nervous.

'What if I don't like him? What if it's awkward? What if he does expect me to have sex with him?'

The next day, she got a text. 'Meet me downstairs. We are going for lunch.'

She went down, very nervous, and sat in the limo. There he was, tall, broad shoulders, with a big bright smile on his face.

'Hi,' he said.

'Hi,' she said.

Oh my God, he was so attractive. Dressed in a casual suit, he looked like George Clooney but with blonde hair.

'Thanks for coming.'

'Thanks for this extravagant date,' she said.

'Oh it's nothing,' he said in a very deep sexy voice. 'Should we go around the Sacré-Cœur for lunch?'

'Sure,' she said, butterflies in her stomach.

They found a cute cafe facing the church. He was very nice and she felt very comfortable. He told her how he used to be a manager for big artists; he represented Limp Bizkit, Backstreet Boys, Snoop Dogg, Enrique Iglesias, Vin Diesel, Ice Cube, Kelly Clarkson, OneRepublic and even Jennifer Lopez.

'How did you get into it?' she asked.

'I was in college and just started representing college bands. I guess I just had a talent to find the best musicians.'

And, soon, he was representing all the biggest musicians in the world. Now, he wanted to be a producer for TV shows. No more artist management for him, he told her.

'Please let me pay for lunch,' she begged when the cheque came.

He laughed. 'No way!'

'Please,' she said. 'You've done so much, it would make me feel better.'

'Okay,' he said finally.

She paid. It was a lot for her but it made her feel better.

That evening, they went to the concert.

They entered through the backstage. They were in the front row. Her chest was thumping to the beat of the music. A chopper landed on stage. A huge inflatable flying pig without testicles plopped down right in front of her. She had goosebumps as the forty-feet wall broke in front of her eyes as people sang 'Another Brick in the Wall'. The sound. The graphics. Everyone singing. The fireworks!

She looked at him, 'I'm having a religious experience.' He laughed, 'I'm so happy seeing you enjoy it.' He was sweet. And then, after the concert, they went to dinner with Roger Waters and his wife in the Louvre. She couldn't believe it. She felt a bit overwhelmed there, not really knowing what to say to Roger Waters, who said to her, 'He's a great guy. Keep him.' She nodded.

It felt unreal. A sexy older lady came up and hugged him, 'Still into twenty-year-olds from the Third World, I can see.'

She was shocked.

He was very embarrassed.

'I apologize for my drunk friend,' he said.

She nodded. She was younger than him and from the Third World, but she wasn't twenty!

They went to a night club after that but she couldn't get that lady's voice out of her head. Maybe she was projecting, but she felt that people were looking at her like she was one of those girls who are with older men for their money. She usually judged those girls. Now she was judging herself.

He asked her to pick a bottle of wine from the menu. She, who was from a middle-class background, couldn't help looking at the prices on the side. *Oh my God*. None of them were under a 1000 Euros.

'They are too expensive,' she said. 'I can't pick.'

He brushed her off and just randomly picked one. She almost choked looking at the price as they sat there with the view of the Eiffel Tower.

He started showing her some videos on his phone.

'Maybe you should watch it on Wi-Fi,' she said. 'This will eat up your data.'

'I don't care,' he said.

She sensed a slight annoyance in his voice for bringing up money for the second time.

His friends came to meet them. He introduced her to everyone, including her in all their conversations.

As they sipped wine, looking at the Eiffel Tower, Lady Gaga walked in, came straight to their table and gave him a kiss. She stood there awkwardly. 'My brother is going to call you, don't say no.'

He laughed and whispered to her, 'She wants me to manage her but I don't want to be a manager anymore. I'm looking forward to just being a producer.' She nodded. *What is this life? Is this all for real?*

He dropped her to her room at the end of the night. She stood on her toes and gave him a hug. He was very attractive and she felt like kissing him but just the fact that he had paid for everything made her stop. *If only he was just a normal guy*, she found herself thinking.

That night when she went to sleep, she wondered if she could be with a man like this. White, older, from a completely different world and so much richer.

The next day, Billionaire flew back to LA and she to New York.

Before leaving, he asked her to come to LA to meet him.

She wrote him a text that read, 'Thank you. That was the best first date I ever had. Unfortunately there's a huge age gap and I don't think this will work.'

She told her roommate Gloria about him as they sat in their tiny New York apartment wondering how she would make next month's rent. Her show had been cancelled and she really didn't know what to do next. Also she had this giant hole in her heart; she was missing Humble and Roller Boy. How could she miss them both?

Gloria first stared at her in disbelief, and then, pointing her manicured nail at her, she said in her South American accent, 'Are you telling me you said no to the billionaire for those two losers?'

No, she said. 'He's just . . . too rich for me.'

'You're saying no to an attractive, tall, sexy billionaire because he's a billionaire?'

She nodded. 'He's from another world.'

Gloria jumped out of her chair. 'Are you crazy? I would kill for this kind of opportunity. I would kill you if I had to and I like you. You can do anything in your life—act in movies, make a movie, live in Beverly Hills, all those environment projects you dreamt of, you can do anything. Are you mad?'

She laughed, 'What is with you South American girls? Why are you so dramatic?'

'You're being a dumb bitch.'

Wow, Gloria was losing it.

'You said no to a self-made billionaire!' Gloria said. 'Girl, you get this opportunity once in your life.'

'Get your ass out of bed and call him. NOW. You know how many girls, including me, have been waiting their whole life for a man like this?'

She laughed. 'So you date him.'

'He wants you. Not me. You are struggling to pay rent with your show being cancelled and all. And you're saying no to this guy?'

'I told him he was too old for me.'

'He's thirteen years older, so f . . . ing what?' Gloria was yelling.

'I told him I was twenty-nine.'

'YOU LIED!' Gloria screamed.

Her phone was ringing.

'It's him,' she said to Gloria.

She answered.

Gloria, 'Put it on speaker.'

'You're the oldest twenty-eight-year-old, born in 1984,' he said.

Gloria whispered loudly, 'Oh my God. He knows when you were born.'

She was quiet, caught in the lie.

He laughed. 'You forgot my secretary booked your ticket. And when she asked me how the date went, I told her you were twenty-eight, and she was like no, she isn't. I have her passport copy.'

'I am sorry I lied about my age,' she said softly.

But instead of being upset, he said, 'Make it up to me. I've bought you a ticket to LA. Come, stay with me in my home in Malibu for a day. We can go to the Laker game and then you can fly back. Just for a day. Second date.'

She was quiet. Gloria was jumping on the sofa.

'Are you not attracted to me?' he asked. 'I can feel our chemistry.'

Gloria was on the sofa, making stabbing actions. 'I will kill you,' she was whispering dramatically.

'It's not that,' she said.

'What is it?'

'I don't know,' she said.

'Okay then, pack your bag. See you tomorrow.'

She hung up.

Gloria started jumping. 'You better be flying me first class everywhere after you're married,' she said.

'I'm not marrying him,' she said.

'You tried settling for love,' Gloria screamed, 'what did it give you? NOTHING! Now it's time to settle for shoes and bags and private jets and a home in Malibu. You will never have to work again!'

'I love working,' she said.

'Oh, what does your career give you?' Gloria screamed standing on the chair.

'My career will never wake up one day in the middle of the night after all my hard work and tell me I'm too old, it doesn't love me anymore and it's choosing a Jewish twenty-nine-year-old.'

Gloria yelled, 'Unless you're an actress.'

'Ugh, unless I am an actress.'

'But you are an actress,' said Gloria emphatically pointing her manicured finger at her. 'You better marry this guy or you will end up old and penniless.'

She laughed. 'What do they feed you in Panama? Why are you so dramatic?'

'What do they feed you in India?' she asked.

'Self-respect,' she said laughing.

'Eff your Indian self-respect. Listen, these kind of opportunities come along only once in your life. If you're lucky. And I want a whole designer wardrobe and you're paying for my boob job too.'

'You already have a boob job,' she said.

'I want them bigger,' Gloria exclaimed holding her boobs. 'My boobs are like my third and fourth eye. They are psychic. And they are telling me I need to help you pack. No, that dress is too long, pick a shorter dress. I've been telling you to come to Panama to get butt implants. That would really seal the deal,' Gloria said.

'What's wrong with my butt?' she said.

'It's too real,' Gloria stated and then started twerking, showing off her butt implants.

'You're crazy but I love you,' she said to Gloria.

The next day, she arrived at LAX airport. There was an older man waiting for her to escort her outside. They waited at the baggage carousel together, not knowing what to say to each other.

Her bag didn't arrive. She was visibly upset.

The man looked at her and snickered, 'Don't worry, little girl; Daddy will buy you a whole new wardrobe.'

She almost choked, wanting to take the next flight home.

The statement stuck with her and really dampened her mood, more than her bag not arriving. And so when she went outside and Billionaire jumped out of his fancy Aston Martin to welcome her, she wasn't feeling so excited.

He spoke to her excitedly as she sat in the front seat with the older man at the back. But somehow, she just couldn't get that awful statement out of her head.

He was so nice. He gave her the entire lower floor of his Malibu house while he stayed on the floor above.

She refused to let him buy her clothes and insisted on going to H&M and buying her own clothes.

That evening, they went to the Laker game, and spotted Leonardo DiCaprio, Kim Kardashian and Jack Nicholson. Some of the basketball players came and high-fived him. He included her in all the conversations, introduced her to all his friends, he was so respectful.

And so the romance started. He would fly her for a game and they would spend a day together in his gorgeous Malibu house, which was right next to Jennifer Aniston's house.

In the morning, she would eat the best Mexican-style eggs with jalapenos and avocado made by his cook. She would chat with the cook about life in Mexico and India while looking out at the ocean dotted with surfers.

She would be part of his fancy life for a weekend and then go back to her crumbling apartment and daily struggles.

He came to New York often too. He owned a whole building in SoHo. It was gorgeous.

'I am a little bored with all the sports,' she told Gloria one day. 'I have been to more than fifteen Knicks games and they haven't won once. The highlight of the games is the all-you-can-eat sushi buffet. And I sometimes find myself fantasizing about the hot basketball players.'

'Are you complaining about going to the Knicks games? While my date is taking me to Mc Donald's? I will kill you if you mess this up,' Gloria said. 'I want my first-class tickets and expensive clothes once you marry him,' she said pointing her manicured finger nails at her.

Once he flew her on a private jet to watch a football game in Ohio. American football. Before the game, he took her to the field to meet the players. She had no idea who they were but was polite and shook their hands. They were quite hot. She had a secret thing for these athletic black guys.

God! she thought, *it's so disrespectful of me to even think that while this guy is going above and beyond for me.*

She fell asleep during the football game, and when she woke up, she asked him, 'Is this the fifth quarter?'

Billionaire laughed. 'There are four quarters,' he said. He thought it was so cute so he told all his friends about it at dinner that night. They all laughed but she could tell they didn't find it as cute. Some of those older white women looked at her with envy. She could feel it.

Her friend Gunjeet was visiting from Delhi. When she told her about Billionaire, she was excited.

'You have a pot of gold,' she told her. 'And since we were kids, boys wanted it. You got to use it. How long will you hustle?'

She laughed, 'Pot of gold!'

'She gives it to the wrong people,' Gloria screamed from the next room. 'Or people like Humble who don't want it. Did you hear Humble was having affairs left, right and centre under her nose through their relationship?'

She started tearing up. 'Oh please, don't start with the waterworks,' Gunjeet pleaded.

'I don't know if I can trust my instincts when choosing a boyfriend anymore,' she said sobbing.

'You want loyalty? Get a dog,' Gunjeet stated coldly flicking her hair.

'Now please, I want to go shopping. Get a husband soon so you can go shopping with me.'

Gunjeet left, making her feel worse rather than better.

She sat on the floor thinking. Was she looking for love in all the wrong places?

One day, Billionaire was walking her home after another meal at a beautiful restaurant. He said something about how he wanted to settle down and have children. She didn't feel comfortable. She missed Humble and Roller Boy.

He could sense her discomfort. 'Every time I mention something serious with us, I feel you stiffen up,' he said.

She stopped walking and looked up at him. 'I feel lost. I don't know if this is the right thing.'

He looked down sadly.

'Maybe I need to be single right now.'

'I feel low and I don't know why,' she said. 'I guess I do know, I found out Humble had other girlfriends while we were together.'

'Let me take you to the Maldives,' he said. 'Wanna go?'

'No,' she replied. 'I can't let you do more for me.'

'I like doing things for you,' he said. 'It makes me happy.'

'It makes me feel like a loser,' she blurted. 'I don't want to be one of those girls who married for money. Some girls feel a lot of power by having a guy who pays for everything, but for me it feels like I am giving up my power.'

'I will allow you to pay,' he said hopefully.

'I need to date more people, people like me,' she said. 'Or maybe I don't need anybody. I am not happy right now.'

He was very hurt. She saw the tears in his eyes.

'I wanted to marry you,' he said.

'I am so sorry,' she said. 'I guess, we are just in different places in our lives,' she said. 'I just got out of two big relationships.'

'But I am offering you the world,' he said, 'and you still miss your skater boyfriend, and your ex who was mean to you and refused to have sex with you?'

She nodded, tears in her eyes.

'I don't know,' she said. 'I find you so attractive but I just don't know. I don't feel we are a good fit. You're amazing but I'm not sure you're my person. And I don't want to be with someone for the great life. I want to be with someone for love.'

'I love you,' he said.

'I guess, I just am not there yet,' she said.

'Okay,' he said, 'I respect that. Maybe you will get there?'

'Maybe I won't?' she said. 'You should go with one of those women from your world,' she said. 'So many of them are crazy about you.'

'I am crazy about you,' he whispered.

'But why?' she said. 'I'm broken. I need time, I need to heal. I need to find myself,' she said. 'I need to date more people before I decide.'

He had tears in his eyes.

He gave her a hug and left. She watched him go with mixed feelings. Would she regret this?

Recipe

Mexican-style eggs

LESSON LEARNT

1. It could be prince charming, but if you're not in a good place in your life, you won't be able to make it work with anyone.

2. If you don't feel you deserve it, you will jeopardize it.

3. Meeting the right guy at the wrong time is like being served the south Indian thaali when you've just finished a mediocre meal and you don't have place for another bite.

WHERE IS HE NOW?

She emailed him a few years later and apologized. He sent her a picture of his blonde wife and blonde baby girl. Gloria is still angry with her.

THREE THANK YOU'S AND A SORRY:

1. She thanks him for the best first date of her life!

2. She thanks him for showing her so much respect, inviting her everywhere and introducing her to all his friends, including Justin Bieber and Lady Gaga, even though she was hesitant and sitting on the fence about them.

3. She thanks him for helping her lose her judgment (even though it's in hindsight) about rich people and see that billionaires can also have billion-dollar hearts.

She is sorry she hurt him and couldn't see the magnificent man that he was because her eyes were clouded with judgment about his age, colour and wealth.

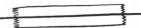

SHE MISSES:

1. His bright smile, the twinkle in his eyes and his kindness.

2. His intelligence and enthusiasm when he spoke about sports and politics.

3. His broad and tall frame.

18

HEALTHY. UNHEALTHY. TOXIC.
WHAT'S YOUR RELATIONSHIP SPECTRUM?

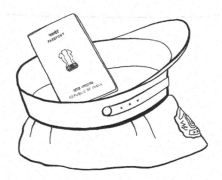

Roller Boy and she sat staring at the sunset in Puerto Rico in silence. They had gone on a holiday together to figure things out. Could they give it a second chance?

Out of the blue, he reached over and pulled a hair out of her head.

'Ouch! What's that for?'

'I have something stuck in my teeth,' he said as he started flossing his teeth with it.

She sighed. Was this her destiny?

They had good chemistry and love but she could feel his bitterness and anger. She didn't entirely blame him. They had been going back and forth for a few years now because she couldn't make up her mind. Was it just in her nature to second guess everything?

He had started to get really jealous, checking her phone and her social media accounts. He somehow always managed to crack all the passwords. She felt she had nothing to hide so she just handed the phone to him and laughed about it.

He snatched her phone, opened it and started typing to Humble. 'STOP,' she said. He kept typing. She snatched it away. 'He's blocked me anyway,' she exclaimed.

A hot girl passed by on roller blades.

'You're bending too much,' he said to the hot girl. She turned.

'Oh my God,' screamed the hot girl, 'I can't believe it's you, the best roller blader in the world! I've been following you since I was a kid. Can you please help me with . . .' Roller Boy got up.

'I'm going to go,' he said to her. He put on his blades and bladed off with the hot girl.

She sat there by the river, with tears in her eyes, staring at the sunset. What was she to do, anyway? He was so bitter and angry with her.

A Puerto Rican woman in her seventies, who had been watching them for some time, leaned in. 'Don't waste your tears dear,' she said.

She looked up, embarrassed.

The older woman said, 'Never have one.'

'I'm sorry, one what?' she asked.

'Never have one man. Take it from me. Your boyfriend, he's a charmer.'

She nodded.

'Well, so are all my boyfriends. And I learnt long ago, with men. Never have one. Have three.'

She couldn't help smiling.

'That's interesting advice,' she said, 'he's already so jealous.'

The woman laughed. 'They are jealous most when they are up to something.'

She frowned.

'One man will always disappoint. Once I learnt that, I never cried again.' And with that, the seventy-year-old woman got up and left.

A few weeks later, they were back in New York. Roller Boy showed up with tears in his eyes, telling her he had missed her.

'Let's give it a real try, I love you too much, I can't stop,' he said.

'Okay,' she replied.

She was house hunting. Her lease was up.

'Move in with me,' he said.

'To the Bronx?' she asked.

'Why not?' he said. 'This is where I am from.'

'Okay,' she said, willing to work on it.

A week later
Time: Midnight
Location: His house, in the Bronx

Roller Boy was already quite drunk. He had been drinking—something he had been doing a lot these days.

She was slurping a strawberry gelato cone. Something she had been doing a lot these days.

Her phone rang, a man's name was on the caller ID. He immediately reached for it. 'You want to sleep with her, huh? Why else would he be calling at this time?' It was a friend from India who never calculated the time difference.

She tried to snatch the phone away. He pushed her. Some of the gelato fell on the bed.

'Look what you have done,' she said, exasperated.

'I don't care,' he said and snatched her cup of gelato and emptied it on the floor.

'Why did you do that? I was enjoying it,' she said.

'Eat it,' he said with a bitter laugh, pointing to the floor.

She pulled the whiskey bottle away.

'You have had too much to drink.'

He pulled the bottle back.

He then proceeded to call every male on her phone to threaten them.

'Call her again, and I will kill you.'

She tried to grab the phone back, but he shoved her away.

She fell, the gelato on the floor soaking her nightie.

He was threatening another guy on the phone.

'You want to fuck her. Don't you? Come here, let me show you how.'

'You're crazy,' she yelled.

She tried to take the phone from him again but he wouldn't let go.

They started wrestling. He was stronger than her and her head hit the cupboard.

She was furious. Crying, she grabbed a bathrobe, ran downstairs, opened the door and walked into the street. It was 2 a.m., and they were in the Bronx. The streets were empty.

She was in a gelato soiled nightie and a bathrobe and fluffy slippers.

Roller Boy yelled from the window. 'Come back. It's not safe. We are in the Bronx.'

She yelled back, 'You're not safe. Give me my phone, pack my clothes, bring them down here. I am leaving you. This time forever.'

He laughed drunkenly, waving the phone out of the window.

'Come get it, baby.'

She sat on the steps. It was cold. Minus 12 degrees. *What was she, a good girl from Bandra, Mumbai, doing in the Bronx in the middle of the night? And where was she to go?* She had left her wallet in the house too. She wondered, 'How did this relationship go from sizzling passion to exasperating drama to outright disrespect? Yes, she was equally to blame but was it time to give up and walk away?'

He came down and sat beside her. She made another futile grab at her phone.

He held her at bay and started calling another number. She tried to wrestle it out of his grasp and almost fell down the stairs in the altercation that ensued. He continued to threaten whoever was on the other end of the line.

Furious, she said, 'I'm going to the cops.' She angrily wiped away her tears and ran down the block.

'Come back,' he yelled.

She kept running. The wind beat against her cheeks. This was a New York City winter, and she was running down the streets in her bathrobe and fluffy slippers. But the adrenaline kept her warm.

She passed some shady characters; a man tried to sell her drugs, a drunk guy waved at her, but she was fine. She felt safer here than on the steps of the house she'd just run away from. Besides, she was a Mumbai girl. *The Bronx at 2 a.m. is way safer for women than India at 2 a.m.*

She knew there was a police station not far from where she was.

She could see it. A few men in uniform were standing outside. *Am I really going to do this?*

A huge white male cop eyed her. 'Everything okay?'

'My boyfriend is drunk and misbehaving. I need to get my stuff, my phone and my wallet and go to my friend's home.'

'Did he hit you?'

'No, but he is bordering on violent. He pushed me.'

'Ma'am, you're going to have to come in and write a report.'

'I won't write a report. Can't you just go with me so we scare him, and I can then get my stuff?'

'Sorry, ma'am. Unless you write a report, we can't do that.'

'Please.'

The desperation in her voice caught the attention of the Puerto Rican cop who had just exited the building. 'I will go with her,' he said.

The big white cop looked at his colleague and then at her. 'It's quite common for women, victims of domestic violence to not want to write reports.'

'I am NOT a victim of domestic violence. I just want my stuff from my drunk boyfriend, and I don't want to go back to the house.'

He relented, and the three of them set out back the way she'd come. Soon, they were standing at the place she called home.

They rang the bell aggressively.

Roller Boy poked his head out of the window.

The cops yelled, 'Come down, Sir.'

Roller Boy looked at her, 'They will beat me up. Is that what you want?'

'I just want my stuff, and I want to go.'

'Come down, Sir.'

'Ma'am, you are going to have to write the report now.'

'If you write that report, they will beat me.'

'I am not writing the report, just pack my bags and get them down. My wallet is on the side table, my passport is in your cupboard and don't forget my phone.'

Roller Boy went inside.

The white cop continued his pursuit of wanting a written report.

'I've seen this guy, he's always jay walking, on roller blades. Write it,' he said.

'No,' she replied firmly.

She stood in the freezing cold, trying to come to terms with this surreal situation.

A few minutes later, Roller Boy poked his head out of the window again.

'Her bag is on the other side of the house.'

The cops went to the back. Roller Boy had jumped out of the back window and put all her stuff neatly in the back and then climbed back up.

'If I come down, they will hit me. You don't know New York City cops like I do.'

She stood there, looking up at him with tears in her eyes. How could a love so strong and passionate have gone so wrong? Is fear the reason we sabotage our great passionate loves?

'I'm sorry,' she yelled up at him, her voice cracking.

His voice too became deeper. He sniffled. 'I'm sorry too. I couldn't do it. I couldn't deal with the jealousy and the pain. I am angry.'

'I understand.' She looked up at the man she loved.

'I love you but I can't stay,' she said.

'I love you but I'm too angry,' he said.

She was overcome with the urge to run up and hug him but she knew it was over. He hadn't been able to forgive her. She had tried, but their relationship had ended the day he had seen the letter from Humble on her laptop in India.

The police led her to a police van. 'Ma'am, do you have somewhere to go?'

'I can go to my friend's home in Columbus Circle.'

'The police van will take you.'

She got into the van with her belongings, still shaken. She was still in her nightie, robe and fluffy slippers. It was freezing cold.

There were other cops in the van and some shady characters too. She half smiled to herself. What an interesting moment. In a cop van with sex workers and drug sellers, driving away forever from the man she loved passionately. She was sure she would never forget this moment. It was printed in her mind forever.

The van drove her to Sonia's house in the well-maintained Columbus Circle area.

She sat in the lobby of the fancy apartment building till the sun came up.

Then, when it was 7.30 am, she went up and rang the bell.

Two days later, she was on her friend Sonia's couch feeling pretty sad and missing him when she got an email from a Japanese girl.

'Roller Boy has been having sex with me, my best friend and a Palestinian girl. He told me if I tell you, he will tell my husband. But I can't take it any longer; please meet me. I'm going to tell my husband myself.'

She was curious. Not thinking of what usually happens to curious cats, she met the Japanese girl who came with her good-looking African American husband. The three of them sat on the grass in the garden. The girl was crying, her husband holding her hand.

'Did he force you?' her husband asked.

'No, I am addicted to the sex,' the Japanese girl said.

She choked. *This Japanese girl was addicted to sex with MY boyfriend!*

'He did it with me in the bathroom at the Standard hotel, he just did it with me everywhere but didn't respect me. He treats me like dirt. And he had so many others. But he loved you and only you,' the girl said turning towards her. 'He kept saying it was revenge sex!'

'Did he force you?' her good-looking husband asked again.

'No,' she said, 'the sex was just too good, I am addicted,' she screamed as she wiped away her tears.

Her husband looked like he was going to cry.

But the Japanese girl was crying loudly now. She held her hand. She couldn't believe it, she was comforting a girl who had been having sex with her boyfriend. (Well, ex-boyfriend but still it had been just two days).

Passersby turned to stare.

She thought of the seventy-year-old woman and what she had said. 'Don't have one. Have three.'

Her phone rang. It was him. She disconnected and blocked his number. It was time to move forward.

RECIPE

*Strawberry gelato
with a good whiskey*

LESSON LEARNT

*1. She learnt that once anger, resentment
and bitterness set in, it's very hard to get
back to what it was again.*

*2. Love thrives on understanding, trust and
respect. Toxicity thrives on power imbalance
and control.*

*3. Love promotes personal growth.
Toxicity will drain you and consume all
your energy, not allowing you to focus on
anything else.*

4. She learnt to recognize the signs of
toxic behaviour:

a. Drama
b. Trust issues
c. Lies and withholding information.
d. Disappearing for days
e. Emotional manipulation
f. Disrespectful behaviour
g. Lack of support
h. Power imbalance
i. Incompatible value system.
j. Complete communication breakdown

5. Being in a toxic relationship is like
consuming spicy chips. They are so addictive
but eventually you feel sick and it drains all
your energy.

WHERE IS HE NOW?

He is happily married to a twenty-four-year-old lingerie model.

All is forgiven now. They follow each other on Instagram and cheer for each other's accomplishments.

They will always have love for each other.

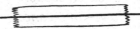

THREE THANK YOU'S AND A SORRY:

1. She thanks him for inviting her into his Harlem Bronx world.

2. She thanks him for re-igniting her inner bad girl.

3. She thanks him for making her feel desirable when she felt like turd.

She is sorry she contributed to making the relationship toxic by going back and forth between Humble and him and not trusting him or her feelings enough to just choose him and go with it.

SHE MISSES:

1. His infectious laugh.

2. Their crazy post-midnight adventures around New York City.

3. Him lifting her up on his shoulders and taking her around town when her feet hurt.

19

Is Sexting the New Love Letter?

New York 2014

She sat on the pot scrolling through Tinder. After Humble, white guys weren't her thing. There were so many white guys on Tinder. An Indian boy's profile popped up. He was not that attractive but she swiped right anyway. It would be nice to meet a sweet Punjabi boy and eat rajma chawal together.

She continued swiping. Swipe left. Swipe left. Swipe . . . wait!

An attractive, very attractive dark man showed up. He was not Indian but he was brown with Will Smith's features. He was wearing a tight grey T-shirt, muscles rippling from under, even in the photo. She scrolled through his other pictures. Skydiving. Mountain climbing. Running a marathon. Wow, he really had a perfect body. Strong calves. Round butt. A six-pack. He was fit and very handsome and adventurous!

Age: Forty-four. Wow, a little older than she would choose but he looked thirty-four! *They say black don't crack and perhaps that's true.*

She swiped right.

It was a match!

She immediately got a message from 'Black Don't Crack'.

'Hey there, are you really the tumbler of firecrackers you appear to be? Spunky and sexy mixed with equal parts of sassy and sweet?'

Not interested in getting into a full-blown text conversation, she wrote, 'Well, there's only one way to find out.'

The next day they met at a bar called Endive in the Upper West Side that served wine and appetizers. She picked a table facing the street. She was sceptical. He was the first person she was meeting from the Internet.

He walked into the bar. Sat next to her. He had a nice face, thick lips, nice smile and really white teeth. She couldn't really see his body in the dark and he looked a little shorter than the six feet that he claimed in his dating profile.

'You're forty-four? You look twenty-four,' she said.

He smiled. 'Gets me into trouble all the time. The twenty-year-old ladies are always trolling me.'

'And you look not a day older than twenty-five,' he said.

'Well at least we know that if we have a child, she will be forever young.'

They both laughed.

They made some more small talk. It wasn't special. She didn't feel any sparks. She sipped her wine, thinking she was ready to go.

He asked if he could walk her home. She agreed. As they walked back to her friend's place, she felt a little attraction from his side. Was he going to try and kiss her? I hope not, she thought. She just wasn't feeling it.

She told him she was busy when he texted her the next day.

A month flew by. He reached out to her, asking her out, but she said she was busy and she was. She was producing her first YouTube show.

Another month went by.

Her phone beeped. It was Black Don't Crack again.

'Would you like to watch *Love Letters* with me tomorrow? I have two tickets.'

The Broadway, she thought. *Why not*?

It was freezing. It was December in New York. It had been four years, and she still hadn't got used to winter, and like most Indians, she still didn't know how to dress for the cold.

She had worn a long sexy dress under two sweaters, a puffy jacket, socks and some ugly flat boots and she was still cold. She passed Forever 21 and stepped in for the heater. She spotted a cute red hat. 'Need that hat, doesn't go with my outfit but it will keep me warm,' she thought. She took it and stood in the line to pay. Fifteen minutes later, she was still in the queue. She glanced at the time; she needed to leave right away. She was late; they wouldn't let her into the show.

She requested the lady behind her to keep her spot in the line, gave her the hat and walked out of the shop.

It was freezing! She ran back in. *That hat will keep me warm.*

The lady behind her was already paying. She tried to get behind her to pay for the hat, but two black ladies behind her started yelling.

Now she was in a fight. 'I was here, I just went out for a minute,' she pleaded. 'You left. Get to the back to Saudi Arabia, bitch.' The other one said, 'Or are you from Pakistan?'

Infuriated, she put the hat on her head, threw the cash on the counter and said, 'Please, I need to go.' The cashier barely nodded and she walked out of the shop.

Sirens started ringing. *Oh MY GOD!*

The tag on the hat was still on.

They thought she was shoplifting. She begged them to go to the counter where she had left the ten dollars. It was a scene. The two black women were looking at her and giggling. She yelled, 'Tell them. Tell them.'

They were quiet. 'But I left some cash on the counter,' she argued. 'They saw me do it. The cashier even nodded.' The cashier shrugged, 'I don't remember,' she said.

'But but, where's the cash? There's no cash here, miss.'

The guards dragged her downstairs and took photos of her. They made her pay a 200-dollar fine for the 10-dollar hat and told her she could never walk into Forever 21 again.

Now she was really late and had a criminal record. At Forever 21! Paying those 200 dollars really hurt. Anyway she was struggling in New York.

She ran from the train into the crowds of 42nd Street, navigating her way on Google Maps, hoping her battery would at least last till she reached the theatre.

She reached just in time and scanned the crowd for a black guy. It had been a couple of months; she didn't even remember what he looked like. She noticed a tall, sexy, well-dressed black man leaning against a car. Her heart skipped a beat. He smiled at her. *Oh my God, is that him? He's hot!* What was she thinking? Why hadn't she followed up with him? And why was he taller? Or maybe it was because her shoes were flat today. She tried to take her jacket off. She knew she looked crazy. And the stupid red criminal hat.

He escorted her into the theatre. She threw off all the layers and stood up, trying to show him her sexy dress. He smiled. The play was about to start. She sunk into her seat thinking about her criminal record. God, she had hit an all-time low. It really was time to go back home to India.

The play was beautiful. For those who don't know, *Love Letters* is about childhood friends who have a lifelong correspondence, despite remaining physically apart, but spiritually as close as only true lovers can be.

After the play, Black Don't Crack took her to the Miss Lily's Jamaican restaurant in the East Village.

'Did you enjoy the play?'

'Loved it,' she exclaimed.

'Are you going to disappear again?' he asked.

She laughed, looking at his muscular shoulders, thinking *Oh God, no*.

'Why don't we write letters to each other?' he asked. 'Handwritten letters, not emails.'

She smiled and nodded. 'Sure,' she said. 'I can write!'

Being half Jamaican, he explained the menu to her. She was only half listening, her eyes were on his shoulders and arms. He stood up to talk to someone; she couldn't help looking at his butt. *Wow, this man has the body of a god*. She felt herself swooning. It had been a while since she had a boyfriend.

She thought she had set the bar high with the Latino Roller Boy but this guy had the face and style of a GQ model with a body that could make Tiger Shroff feel bad.

They made a plan to write a love letter to each other before every meeting.

She soon realized it is hard to write a letter to someone you don't know at all.

She scribbled something down five minutes before meeting him on the subway. But was embarrassed when he placed a carefully written letter in her hand. It even smelled good. Had he sprinkled cologne on it? He nodded.

The letter read, 'I don't know if this love story will last one year, two years, a decade or forever but I have a feeling it will span across countries and continents.'

And so the love story with Black Don't Crack began.

He worked in Queens all day but came to her small place in the West Village every night. They ate, they laughed and spent all their free time together. The weekends were her favourite part—they had epic brunches, they went to Central Park and they checked out museums together. It was nice being with someone as energetic and interested in doing the same things as her. He was always up for exploring the city with her and they discovered art galleries, concerts in the park and off-Broadway shows together. Their favourite thing was getting a peanut butter acai bowl from Juice Generation on West 4th Street and then walking to Washington Square Park. They had FUN!

He wasn't lazy like Humble or busy like Roller Boy; he was always enthusiastic about doing things with her. Summer rolled into winter. They were still together. Her plans of moving back home to India were on the back burner. He wrote her beautiful texts and letters. He had a flair for writing.

'Why do we need to write letters when we see each other every day?' she asked.

'I love words,' he said.

She wrote him letters and texts back but didn't really put her heart into it. After all, she was seeing him at night anyway.

One day, as she was sitting in a coffee shop, happy and in love, she googled his name.

SHOCK!

She froze.

Shaking, she asked him that night. 'You spent eleven months in jail?'

He calmly sat her down. They called it embezzlement; he called it kickbacks. He said he regretted it. It was way back in his past, he paid for it by going to jail.

They turned the lights off. She lay next to him in the dark. She was with a man who had been to jail. She came from such an honest family. Her family never even bought a movie ticket in black.

She was planning to leave New York and go back to India in a few months. This relationship would die a natural death then. Till then, it was nice to have some companionship and a very hot companion at that. It was lonely in New York, especially in the cold. And she had grown really fond of him. She stayed with him but with some apprehensions.

She also found out from Google that he used to be a ramp model back in the day and had travelled all over the world—Paris, Milan. She wasn't surprised. That body. But he wasn't just a body, he was extremely smart and creative too.

But why was he always so quiet about himself? He loved hearing her stories but he rarely shared. She had to push him to talk about himself.

Now it made sense. The criminal record was the reason why he wasn't able to get a good job and worked for a small Jamaican radio station when he could be heading NBC.

'What was it like in jail?' she asked him.

God! What was it about her and bad boys?!

'We fell into a routine. I worked in the canteen, I worked out, we read, watched films and eleven months went by. My sister came every week to see me. Honestly, the months leading up to it were more traumatic, when they found out I had been taking kickbacks. It was a Bloomberg company; they wanted to make an example of me. It could be because I'm black. I spent all my savings on courts and lawyers.'

'In the article they said you got off easy, you could have been in there for eleven years.'

He nodded, no expression on his face. That was the thing about him. He always had the same expression. She never really knew how he felt. 'Why did you do it?' she asked.

'Because I thought I could get away with it,' he replied.

She thought about herself and the red hat, throwing the money on the counter and walking off. Guess good people do stupid things on impulse, because they think they can get away with it.

It didn't sit well with her. But she didn't leave him.

She was leaving New York in a few weeks for India forever, so it didn't matter.

But, one day, while she was in her storage, sweating and packing bags, her phone rang. She had unexpected news. She was selected as one of the contributors on the Nightly Show on Comedy Central, produced by Jon Stewart (*The Daily Show* guy)! A huge job. She couldn't believe it; she had auditioned for that four months ago.

Her plans changed overnight. New York didn't want her to leave. Neither did he; he was overjoyed.

They continued on their journey together. It was good, she was enjoying the adventures around the city but he was very tight lipped about himself.

One year turned into two years.

Their relationship was losing its initial lustre just like all relationships do after a year. She noticed that he wasn't excited to do things together as much as before.

But he was a good boyfriend. He listened to her stories, he helped her read lines for her auditions, he picked her up from the airport, he still went with her to art galleries and museums but not as much. Their epic two-day weekends exploring the city were replaced with him watching football on his phone.

The comedy show she was working on had ended. Auditions weren't working out. She was struggling. Again!

One day, she realized, she couldn't even make rent. She had two options, move back to India or move in with him.

He didn't seem super keen on her moving in but he also didn't want her to move to India. So she moved into his tiny apartment in Brooklyn. Her career was at an all-time low.

He was struggling too; nobody wants to give a good job to someone with a criminal record. So, he worked a job for which he was overqualified. But they were very compatible in their interests and lifestyle and they made good housemates. She woke up every day with him, they made breakfast together and went for a run in Prospect

Park. One day, he came home with a recipe book that someone had left outside their building.

She looked at it.

'All He Left Me Was a Recipe,' she said to him excitedly.

'What's that?' he asked.

She had this idea of a book, a girl discovering herself through all her relationships. She had no publisher and had never written a book but her acting career was not keeping her that busy and she just needed to be creative. He loved the idea and encouraged her.

Someone told her about an app called Instagram. When she was not writing, she was making videos of New York City and uploading them on the app. She started getting a following just for her New York City pictures and videos. He encouraged her with this too.

When he came home at night, he wanted to play a game of cards with her. She often asked why they couldn't just talk but he liked to play and talk so she just gave in.

Their life wasn't as exciting as before. They weren't able to afford all the fun stuff they were doing before since her show had been cancelled.

Is this what her life had become? She thought she would have an exciting life in New York City but the highlight of her evening was a game of cards.

Even on weekends, which used to be so much fun before, he was not keen. It was football season and all he wanted to do was watch the game and play fantasy football.

She started noticing things like his eyes were just blank. He couldn't make eye contact for too long with her. Strange, she hadn't noticed this before. Guess they were always doing stuff together, side by side so she hadn't noticed. His eyes were just dead. The only time she really saw some expression was when he looked at food. 'I wish you looked at me like you look at eggs Benedict,' she joked.

And while everything else seemed great—they were the perfect looking couple, they had similar interests, explored the world together, laughed at each other's jokes, supported one another, encouraged each other—a small voice told her something was wrong.

Maybe I am just missing India, she told herself and dismissed the voice in her gut.

She never quite felt she could really get him to be vulnerable and open with her. He looked her in the eye but not for long. They talked but only while walking around a museum or playing a game of cards. There always had to be something else. And when they smooshed, he closed his eyes.

She told her friend Sonia, 'Couples usually fight about the same things through the relationship. You either work through those things or those things break you apart. With Humble, it was the lack of physical intimacy. With Roller Boy it was his jealousy.'

With Black Don't Crack, it was:

1. Bathroom: He spent an unusual amount of time in the bathroom. And they had only one in the tiny apartment. And if she knocked, he got really really angry. That was the only time he ever got angry. It scared her. She was always peeing in a glass out of desperation.

2. When they travelled, he wanted her to shoot pictures of him alone in iconic places. Maybe it came from him being a model in the past. She didn't mind taking the pictures; he was after all a hot guy and a good model and she loved taking photos, but she just found it strange that he asked for pictures of himself and never tried to take pictures of them together. He also never put up pictures of them together on Facebook, just his, by himself, like she didn't exist. And when she asked about it, he called her childish.

3. Pictures of ex-girlfriends in the house that he refused to put away. 'It's part of my history,' he said. But they were also still in his life as his best friends. She felt she was becoming the insecure one in this relationship. She tried to brush off the feeling. She didn't want to be the jealous girlfriend.

4. Clutter. The apartment was full of stuff. Old magazines, old photos, clothes from 1999 and junk. Stuff that they just didn't need. The clutter made her crazy, she was a minimalist.

She quietly threw out a few old GQs from 2001. One day she threw out some extra pillows. But he spotted them in the garbage and brought them back to the house.

'Why do we need so much stuff?' she argued.

'It's part of my history,' he insisted.

'This old pillow?' she asked puzzled.

She dared not ask him again about the ex-girlfriends' pictures. She couldn't say much as she had moved into his house.

But she started voicing her concern with his going out to meet his ex-girlfriends every Wednesday. That seemed to be 'ex-girlfriend night'. He told her she was being a child. She tried to brush it away, but she didn't feel too good.

They slept in the same bed but had stopped spending a lot of time in the day together. He was at work all day while she sat in coffee shops by herself and wrote her book. The book that she didn't know would make it to the shelves. But she enjoyed writing stories and it was therapeutic for her. Summer turned into winter and winter moved into summer and back into winter. When they romanticize New York, they often forget to mention its never-ending winters, high rents and the relentless round-the-clock hustle required just to survive in this city.

She thought about her plans to move back to Mumbai a lot. New York was so cold. She was so lonely. But if she left it would be over with him.

But was he worth staying for?

Well, he was still doing everything right. He always picked her up at the airport. Called in the middle of the day to see how she was doing. Made soup for her if she wasn't well. They smooshed every night or morning but with his eyes closed.

She brought it up but he said he felt more when his eyes were closed. How could she force him to look into her eyes while they smooshed? But she wasn't enjoying it, it was like she was smooshing just for the sake of it with no connection. It was lonely.

She couldn't find anything to really fight about. But something inside her just wanted to yell at him. 'Are you a robot?'

As time went on, they stopped spending all weekends together. He stopped coming to bed at the same time.

He was really into fantasy football and 'Words with Friends' (a Scrabble app). He stayed up all night talking on the phone. She started getting lonelier. It was so hard to even have good friendships in New York.

One day, she was in an Uber crossing the Brooklyn Bridge. The Pakistani Uber driver was telling her about how he came to America.

'Do you like it here?' she asked.

'If the situation was better in my country, I would go back tomorrow,' he said.

She looked at the beautiful view, the glitzy buildings that had at one time excited her. Now all of that didn't mean anything. In fact, the view that was once the best she had ever seen felt cold and lifeless.

'Why are you here?' he asked.

She found herself choking on her words. Tears rolled down her cheeks. The lights from the Brooklyn Bridge went out of focus. 'My . . . my boyfriend . . . I guess . . .' she said.

'He's a lucky man I am sure,' said the driver. 'Hope he knows that.'

'The thing is,' she said. 'I don't think he realizes that,' she said to herself. And it came to her.

It was time.

She was done. She was going to leave. She was going home to India. To sunshine. To warmth. To smiley faces. And happier people. She couldn't stay another day with him, smooshing with his eyes closed. She felt like she was living with a robot.

She felt more of a connection with the Pakistani Uber driver than her boyfriend. 'You take care now, I think you should go to your country,' he said to her as she walked away teary eyed.

'Thank you,' she mumbled.

He came home that evening. She had made some fish and rice. And as they sat eating, she blurted out, 'I want to move back home.'

'This is your home,' he said expressionless.

'This?' she said looking around at the clutter. The dark apartment. The gentrified neighbourhood of Brooklyn. The pictures of his African American family and friends that stared at her from the frames. The wintry sky, the brick walls of Brooklyn.

'No,' she said. 'This is NOT my home. It is your home.'

She burst into tears. 'I can't do New York anymore. I don't feel like I connect with anybody here. In fact I am always in people's way. I stepped on a woman's foot today and got yelled at. Yesterday a woman on a train got mad at me because my arm touched her, in a crowded train! And when I pass *Hare Krishnas* on the street, the WHITE *Hare Krishnas*, not even the Indian ones, I have tears pouring out of my eyes, just hearing them sing. I need to go home. I'm going home. I'm so sorry . . . I'm leaving New York. I'm leaving this snow. This cold. This clutter.'

'You're leaving me?' he asked.

'But you already left me a while ago. You stopped doing things with me, you zoned out, you're always on your phone, it's like you left me, without physically leaving me,' she said her eyes tearing up.

'You don't even eat acai bowls or go to Washington Square Park with me anymore. I eat them alone! I walk alone. I am just alone! You have already left me. So now, I'm physically leaving you. Sorry.'

Pause. The room went silent.

'What will you do there?' he said.

'What am I doing here?' she said.

'But your acting career,' he said. 'You said you won't get acting jobs in your country. At least here you are acting.'

'I don't want to go to another audition. I can't.'

'But you are getting roles here.'

'So what?' she said. 'A small role in a big film and then what? Nothing for six months.'

'It's just a matter of time,' he said. You have been on some pretty big shows on ABC and Comedy Central and TBS.'

'Okay, so? What does it mean? I don't care. I want out! I want to go to my home. I'm done with America and Donald Trump and being an outsider and a minority.'

'You won't have work there,' he said.

'I will figure it out. I just want to go back to MY COUNTRY! To see people I grew up with, I want to hear people speaking in Indian accents, I want to smell the samosas and sewage. I want to see my parents every day for lunch. I want to be around my nephew. I am DONE here! I am going home.'

Another long pause.

Then:

'I will go with you.'

Silence.

'What?'

'I will move to India with you,' he said.

'But . . . but . . . what about your job? What will you do there? And and . . . Are you even happy with me?'

'We have invested so much time together, I'm not letting you go . . .' he said.

'But your job . . .'

'I lost my job . . .'

'What? When? And when were you going to tell me?'

'Doesn't matter,' he said.

'But it does matter,' she argued. 'What happened?'

'I don't want to discuss it,' he insisted. 'I will move with you.'

'Wow, you're really going to move to India with me? You're a black guy from Brooklyn . . .'

He shrugged. The same dead pan expression.

'There are no black men in India. Or women.'

He shrugged again.

'Indian people are quite racist. They respect the white people but they called back people "kallu".'

'I love you,' he said.

A warmth came over her. *He really loves me.*

'You really love me.'

He nodded.

'I will move to India with you,' he said, matter-of-factly.

They hugged. She kissed him. He kept his eyes open.

'You keep your eyes open when we smooch but close them when we smoosh.'

'What's the problem with that?' he asked.

She shrugged. 'I don't know. It's me. Maybe it's just me.'

A month later, they moved to India. Bandra, where she grew up. Now, the most expensive address in Mumbai. But they were still paying less than half of what they were paying in Brooklyn. It was a big sunny two-bedroom.

And suddenly they were happy again. They were hanging out with her family. Doing up their new apartment together.

They had chosen an apartment with two bathrooms. No more bathroom fights. And all his stuff was in storage. No more clutter!

She was happy. He even opened his eyes sometimes when they smooshed.

She was HOME! It had been too long. She found her smile again. All the things that had bothered her about India when she was younger didn't matter anymore. She sang in traffic jams and laughed when someone honked. Life was good.

They made a plan. Her Instagram with her travel videos was getting some traction. Her followers had grown to 20,000 just with all the New York videos.

Their plan was that they would travel together, he would help her shoot and they would build this page together and be a travel content creator couple. She laughed thinking, 'This was the third boyfriend she was attempting to make a travel show with. Hope it's third time lucky.'

It was so exciting! A brand-new life for them!

She didn't mind breaking her FDs and paying for everything until he got a job or 'maybe this content creation thing paid both of them,' as he suggested.

She laughed.

'You think Instagram will pay our bills? HOW? I don't even know how people make money off this app.'

He shrugged. 'Me neither.'

They went on a family trip to Thailand with her family. Her aunts were not happy with him. 'What is our beautiful girl doing with this blackie?'

'PLEASE DO NOT BE RACIST.' She fought with her family till they had no choice but to accept him. 'He is my man, we are a couple and you have to accept this.'

She loved him more now. He seemed more present.

He was even spending less time on his phone. Or was he?

He was never there when she woke up in the morning.

He was always in the second bedroom which they had converted into an office. At 4 a.m., at 6 a.m.

'It's jetlag,' he explained.

'But we left America two months ago,' she exclaimed. 'Why don't we wake up together?' she said.

'I need less sleep than you,' he replied.

She laughed. She was laughing all the time these days! Oh why had she not moved back earlier?

It was just before Valentine's Day. They were back in Mumbai. He had to go back to New York for some work, he said.

'But it's Valentine's Day,' she said that night as he got dressed for the airport.

He was exceptionally affectionate with her that morning and they smooshed twice (with his eyes open).

'Why do you have to leave two days before Valentine's?'

'Every day is Valentine's for us,' he said.

'This move really helped us,' she said laughing. 'We have life back in our relationship, and no more fantasy football.'

'I don't think you should be happy about that,' he said. 'It's what I enjoy.'

'Sorry,' she said.

They hugged.

'When I am back, we will go on the Golden Chariot train together,' he said.

'Yes,' she replied.

She dropped him to the airport. They kissed a long, deep kiss.

An older man looked at him and said, 'She really loves you. Better come back soon.'

They both smiled. Their eyes locked. Eye contact, not an easy thing for him. She was happy.

She watched him as he walked right in and then went back home.

Life couldn't be better. She was back home with her family. Her relationship was finally where she wanted it to be. Now if only they could figure out how to make money with this Instagram thing, life would be perfect. Her savings were going to last three more months and then what? She would figure it out. She smiled.

She changed his name on her phone to 'my sweet love'. She put a cute picture of the both of them as her WhatsApp display picture.

She took his old iPad that they used to play Spotify, connected it to the speakers and played music. Suddenly it stopped. *God, these speakers are so unpredictable. Or wait, is it the iPad?*

A text popped up. She opened it casually.

WHOA!

It was a dick pic.

It was his dick. From the airport?

Maybe this is an old text, she thought. This was his old iPad.

She put it down.

Should she even be looking at this? But curiosity got the better of her. She picked up the iPad again.

He had sent it to Danielle Nicolette Garcia. Who was Danielle Nicolette Garcia?

One of his exes?

Her eyes glanced on the date.

But wait . . .

She started shaking. The date was 4 January 2018. That was that year!

She ran to the kitchen.

Is that the kitchen floor? No it's the second bedroom floor . . . It's the floor of the apartment. Their apartment! That she was paying rent for!

She dropped the iPad. She was breathing a lot faster. This was not real. This was a mistake.

She needed to call someone but who could she call at midnight? Surely not all her married girlfriends. They wouldn't even know what a dick pic was.

She called her only single friend, Malika. It was midnight but thank God for girlfriends.

'Malika?' she was crying, shaking. 'I don't . . . I don't know what to do. I mean. It's his dick. It's our home. It's 4 January.'

'Text the number,' Malika said calmly. 'Pretend to be him.'

'What?'

'Do as I say,' Malika said.

So she did . . .

'Hello,' she typed.

'Hi, aren't you on the flight?' the stranger/Danielle wrote back.

'Oh my God, Malika, who is this? How does she know?'

'Ask her when are we meeting,' Malika said.

She couldn't breathe.

'Emirates has Internet. When are we meeting?'

'Valentine's Day,' the stranger said.

'Where?' she wrote back.

'Didn't you book the hotel?' the stranger asked. 'Wait, is that YOU?'

'Yes of course,' she said.

'You sound strange,' said the stranger.

'Who else could it be?' she said.

'You could be HIS girlfriend,' the stranger replied.

'I am his girlfriend,' she said, tears pouring out of her eyes, her eyes trembling.

'Who are you?'

Silence

'WHO ARE YOU?' she screamed ON TEXT.

'You should ask your boyfriend that,' the stranger replied.

'How long has this been going on?' she asked.

'We've never met in person. We've been talking for two years. Met on Words with Friends on Valentine's Day two years ago when you were travelling in Bali, shooting your Instagram videos.'

'You met on the freaking Scrabble App? And how do you know everything about me and my travels?'

'We are very close, I have a lot to thank your boyfriend for,' the stranger texted.

'It's because of him I am a nurse, he helped me choose my life path. I met him when I was just twenty-two, I am twenty-four now.'

She was shaking, twenty-four!

'You're a child,' she said.

She burst into tears. 'Calm down,' Malika instructed.

'She's twenty-four, Malika!' she screamed to Malika who was patiently still hanging on the other line.

'Twenty-year-old girls,' Malika said coldly. 'They are all cute until they run away with our men.'

'Call him but don't tell him you know.'

She called him on video call. He was in transit in Dubai on his way to New York.

He looked handsome, wearing yellow sunglasses.

'Hi sweetheart,' he said.

'Who's Danielle?' she came straight to the point, not able to stick to Malika's plan.

He paused. That robot expression was back.

'Never heard that name before,' he said.

'I know everything,' she said. 'I saw the dick pic you sent her.'

Tears poured out of her eyes. Her hands were shaking. He took off the sunglasses, lowered his voice and said, 'Sorry. She's so insignificant. Just some stupid girl who kept pestering me to send a dick pic so I caved in the end and just sent it.'

'What? You sent your dick pic to some girl who pestered you? Where did you meet her?'

'On the Scrabble app, Words with Friends. Please let me come home and explain.'

'I don't trust you,' she screamed.

'I am sorry. I want to mend this,' he insisted.

She hung up, shaking.

She walked around the house, throwing their photo frames on the floor, glass shattering everywhere.

She picked the iPad from the floor. Her hands were trembling. If the FBI were made entirely of women, no crime would go unresolved, because if a woman wants to know, she will find out.

She found his 'Words with Friends' password and entered the chatroom. All his chat history was right there.

Him: Okay, I'm going back to sleep now. Stop distracting me with thoughts of effing you.

Her: Went for a much-needed jog, my panties are so moist. I'd let you smell them if you were here.

Him: Yum

Her: I'm going to take a bath now and pleasure myself with thoughts of you.

Her: What was it like when you were in jail?

Him: The hardest part was not having sex. It's there that I got into the habit of masturbating quietly, that I can't stop now.

Her: Well when you meet me, you will stop.

Him: You should plan on being in NYC from 9 to 12 Feb so we can meet up on our Valentine's Day deadline. I'll arrange the accommodations. You show me what happened in those dreams.

Him: Sometimes the phone is on the table in plain sight. If she finds out. I will have to come live with you indefinitely.

Her: I'm shaved like a landing strip. Waiting for your jumbo jet to land on it.

Him: Oops she's here. She made me a thaali (a big Indian plate full of different dishes).

Her: Sounds delicious. But not as delicious as my wet panties.

Him: You're going to get me caught. Got to go.

Him: Sex with her is not bad. I wish you could join us in bed.

Her: Sure, I would love a threesome, your girlfriend is quite hot.

Him: She would never.

Her: I would. Send me a pic of the two of you. That's going to make me cum tonight.

Him: Ok.

She threw the iPad on the floor. It didn't break. She threw it again. Not a crack.

Black don't crack?

She felt like throwing up.

She picked up the iPad again and she knew it was destructive but she couldn't help herself.

Him: I'm in Thailand for business, wish I could take you.

She was so hurt; she had taken him to Thailand with her family, and he was writing to this chick even from there?

All the photos he had insisted on her taking of him alone, they had all been sent to her in the chats.

But there was more. She discovered that he was reaching out to many random women on the Internet, telling them he was a businessman, travelling around the world. She and he had gone on those trips together.

Who was he? She was living with a man whom she did not even know. What was this split personality?

She lay on the floor in shock, crying, angry, sobbing next to the broken glass frames. That feeling when you don't even feel you deserve to sleep on the bed. How could she have been so blind? Who was he? Who was this man she had been living with for four years? She thought she knew him. But can we ever truly know somebody?

She scribbled in her notes, 'This relationship ended up being faker than my knockoff Gucci bag bought on a New York City street corner. It has more pretence than a Bollywood red carpet event.'

That was the night she felt everything in her life was over.

With her eyes closed, she floated between consciousness and unconsciousness.

The doorbell rang a few hours later. He was standing there, his expression robotic. He had taken the flight back from Dubai.

He stood outside the door and said solemnly, 'You stopped writing me love letters.'

'But we live together,' she said.

'Sorry,' he said. 'I let myself get distracted by another woman. Words, they stimulate me.'

'Words stimulate you?? So, you had an affair on WORDS WITH FRIENDS? How did I not know? How did I not have the slightest intuition? These messages go back two years. Every single day,' she said quietly. 'Who are you?'

'That's why we always fought about the bathroom. You were getting off on "words" while I peed in a glass?

'And that's why you wanted to always have pictures by yourself. So you could send it to strangers on the Internet and tell them you're a rich businessman. Meanwhile, I was taking you on those trips.

'And when I asked you about jail, you just told me you didn't want to talk about it. What was it? Why couldn't you talk to me? But you discussed it with a stranger on the Internet whom you've never met. She could be a man. Is she even a real woman?'

'I feel it's easier to talk to strangers than people I know,' he said.

His phone beeped. She grabbed it and threw it out of the window. They were on the fifth floor.

He sighed and sat on the floor. 'I guess I deserve that,' he said. He didn't seem to care that his phone was out of the window.

'I hate it. I hate myself. I am an addict. It's like being a porn addict. I was addicted to this girl like she was my porn.'

'But you were on your way to meet her,' she said. 'On Valentine's day!'

'It's all a stupid fantasy in my head,' he said.

'What else?' she said. 'Is there anything else that I don't know about you??'

He looked down. 'I am scared of it. But since I am coming clean, you should know. I fantasize about women I see on the street, on the train, anywhere. It could be the way their hair is touching their neck or their bra strap sticking out. So when we are together in bed at night I may think of them while I am with you.'

She choked. 'So you're saying there are other women in bed with us?'

'Yes,' he said. 'I don't know how to stop that. I feel so guilty. But, I just don't know how.'

'That's why your eyes are always closed,' she mumbled.

'It's not that I don't find you attractive, it's just me becoming a fantasy addict.'

'And my friends? Did you fantasize about my friends too?'

He looked down. 'It's a sickness,' he said.

'Oh my God, you have to leave.'

'I want to resolve this,' he said.

'I don't even know you,' she said. 'I feel I have been living with a sick man.'

'I will get help,' he said. 'I will see a therapist. In fact, I was seeing one in New York earlier.'

'And, of course, I had no idea,' she said. 'Because I know NOTHING about a man I was living with for four years!'

'Please, don't take this on you. I am just unhappy with my life. You are the only happy thing in my life.'

'I am not happy,' she said.

'Please,' he begged.

'She was a fantasy. An obsession. You are my reality,' he pleaded.

'Yes, I am a reality. A reality that you didn't introduce to your fantasies,' she said.

'I let myself become distracted with another woman. And women!'

'Distracted?' she said. 'Or obsessed?'

'Yes, I became obsessed,' he admitted. 'But that was only to escape myself. NOT YOU.'

She was sobbing. 'She is twenty-four. She's a girl. Not a woman.'

'I'm a troubled person. I guess have a fantasy addiction. Can you just treat it like a porn addiction?

'I find life is easier and better in my fantasies. It's because I can't get a real job that I deserve. My one mistake in life cost me everything. I love you. Please believe me. I fantasize to make my pain go away. I fantasize to make my life more exciting. I'm in so much debt from the court cases and the lawyers. I just fantasize to forget all the bad stuff in my life.'

He kept saying, 'She was my fantasy, you're my reality.'

She cried. She was also confused. 'I'm sorry. I half feel bad for you but I can't go on living with a man I do not know. You have the ability to lie so easily. I mean, I didn't even suspect that there was someone else. I guess, I had an intuition something was wrong,' she said, 'but . . . I didn't trust it.'

'You're breaking up with me over someone I have never met,' he insisted.

'Someone you spoke to every day. And you enjoyed deceiving me with her. And all those other women you reached out to, making yourself sound important? You have a dual personality.'

'I do,' he said.

'And what about the girls in your head that come to bed with us every night?' she said.

Tears rolled down his cheeks. This was the first time she had seen some emotion from Mr Robot.

'It's something I am working on with a therapist. I hate it. I don't want to do that.'

She hugged him. She empathized with him.

'I love you,' he said.

'Why did you do it?' she asked. 'Why didn't you even say anything about it to me?'

'I guess I thought I could get away with it,' he said.

This was the same answer he had given when she had asked him why he had embezzled money.

'You must leave in the morning,' she said, her eyes full of tears.

'You're angry,' he whispered.

'I am more angry with myself for making a red dupatta from all the red flags. The shock is more disturbing than the actual cheating. I feel I betrayed myself by being so blind. I am blind. How will I trust myself to make the right decisions again? You have to go.'

'I don't have money for a ticket back.'

'Ask your Internet girlfriends,' she said.

They slept. In the morning, she woke up to him offering her eggs Benedict in bed.

'Change your mind?' he asked.

She shook her head.

'My sister paid for my ticket,' he said.

His bags were packed. She walked him down to the Uber. He sat in the car. She waved. He waved. Then, his eyes turned blank again. It was as if a mask had come over his face.

She stood on the street sobbing. The Uber drove off. He didn't look back.

The next day, she packed her bags and went on the Golden Chariot Train, alone. She poked her head out of the train, put on a brave smile and took a selfie.

She captioned it, 'Eff the travel couple thing, I will do this solo.'

She hit post.

Then she burst into tears.

RECIPE

Peanut butter acai bowl

LESSON LEARNT

He cheated to escape
himself. NOT her.
Be with someone
who is happy with
themselves.
Do not make a laal
dupatta out of red flags.

WHERE IS HE NOW?

In Jail?
At the therapist's?
With Danielle Nicolette Garcia?
She has no idea.

But all is forgiven and she wishes they were friends.

THREE THANK YOU'S AND A SORRY:

1. She thanks him for encouraging her to write the book.

2. She thanks him for helping her with auditions no matter how tired he was.

3. She thanks him for taking her to so many off and on Broadway shows and musicals.

She is sorry she told his friends and family about what he did which caused him a lot of shame.

SHE MISSES:

1. Going to their favourite Japanese restaurant together after the Broadway shows and ordering everything.

2. Walking through Washington Square Park with him on Sunday afternoons after digging into the PB smoothie bowls.

3. Laughing and singing loudly with him at home after a musical.

20

In this World of Options, is Monogamy Too Much to Expect?

She texted her friend Gunjeet, 'You're in Mumbai. Come over to my new apartment. Stay here, spend the night.'

Her friend Gunjeet texted, 'Do we have anything to even talk about? I mean, I just can't be friends with someone who isn't married or has kids. What do we even have in common anymore?'

She was shocked. Betrayal from men was one thing but a text like that from her childhood friend . . .

But then was she ever truly a friend or someone who was around to make her feel bad about herself?

She wrote back, 'Single doesn't mean I have a lack of options, it means I am strong enough to leave what is not right for me and not settle for anything less than I deserve.'

No reply.

She texted again, 'And I'd rather be single and adventurous than married and bored.' She hit send.

And then she blocked her! It was time to establish boundaries, even with friends.

Her Instagram business had really taken off. She had put all her energy into it after Black Don't Crack left. She couldn't believe it, but she was starting to get paid for her videos.

She travelled a lot to escape the pain, and while she felt joy while travelling and making videos, she still lay awake at nights.

She couldn't shake off that empty feeling in the mornings so she went to the gym as soon as she woke up. She put the treadmill on 9.1 and ran. She simply ran. She was different these days. She didn't make eye contact with people like she usually did. She didn't smile at anyone. She simply ran. Her tears mixed with her sweat, and she was thankful nobody could see the difference.

Be careful of me by Cardi B played in the background.

She had run till the point of exhaustion. Her heart was beating faster than normal. She felt better. She felt she was now ready to start the day. And this was her daily routine.

She bent over, trying to catch her breath. Her eyes spotted a tall caramel-skinned 'chocolate mocha' man. He was stretching. 'What is that you're using to stretch?' she said. Wow! Did she just speak to him? She had surprised herself.

He looked up and smiled. He had a sweet, genuine smile, *and* he made eye contact. He started explaining the stretching technique and what he was using but she wasn't listening. He seemed nice, she thought.

'You try now,' he said.

'Huh? Er okay.'

He got up to help her.

She was distracted by his beautiful brown skin, his arms and chest muscles rippling under his white T-shirt.

She was on the floor, and he was standing on top of her. Their eyes met. A current passed through her body. She quickly looked away.

He asked for her number. The next day they met at a cafe. He was dressed differently, jeans, chappals, a shirt with some big lettering on it. He had a fanny pack around his waist.

'I shouldn't be superficial about the way he dresses,' she told herself firmly.

He talked loudly. He told her something about running the small shops on Linking Road. He said he had dropped out of college . . . not the usual guy she was attracted to with the fancy USC education. She looked around. People were also listening. She wished he spoke softer. His nose seemed bent, she hadn't noticed that yesterday and he smelled of some cheap cologne. His phone rang; he picked up in one ring and started discussing some business deal loudly.

He offered her a bite from his chocolate mousse. She declined. 'I don't eat sugar,' she said. 'No sugar!' he exclaimed loudly, some spit flying across the table. Kim Arora with her long fake nails and designer bag next to them jumped and gave her a look like 'Who's this guy?' She was embarrassed.

This was certainly not going to happen. What was she even thinking? She went to the counter, asked for the bill and put down her credit card.

He looked surprised but didn't argue.

He walked her home. As it started raining, his voice got softer. He told her about how he came from a conservative Muslim family. 'My dad once followed me in a rickshaw, I was on my scooter and he followed me and watched me hanging out and smoking with my guy friends. And then when I was taking a drag, we suddenly made eye contact. I started coughing and my dad told the rickshaw wallah, 'Chalo chalo'. Then I sat on my scooter and chased him back home.' She laughed and looked up in his eyes for the first time that evening. The current came back. He was actually quite funny, and he seemed smarter than he looked.

He told her he was thirty. She told him she was thirty-seven. And when they got to the gate and he asked when he could see her again, she said never. 'A seven-year age gap is a lot,' she said. But it wasn't the age gap. They were from different worlds. This was not a Bollywood movie; this was real life. She couldn't date this man child who still lived at home and had his dad following him in a rickshaw.

She went home.

The next morning, she woke up to her phone beeping. It was him.

'Good morning, I was thinking about you (with a kiss emoji),' the message read.

It made her smile. She texted back saying, 'It's not happening.'

He persisted. He texted her every morning, starting with the same good morning message and kiss emoji.

She saw him at the gym. They seemed to always be there at the same time. Was he following her? But she liked the attention. She liked how simple and uncomplicated he was.

They ran together, then stretched together. Their eyes met. And she shivered. He was complimentary and attentive.

'It's NOT happening,' she kept telling him laughing. 'You're a kid.'

'Look at Priyanka and Nick,' he persisted. 'They have a ten-year age gap.'

He followed her around the gym, correcting her form as she lifted weights; they laughed. His eyes wouldn't leave hers. She could tell he was very attracted to her. His body was always mirroring hers. She felt her power coming back. She felt attractive and desirable around him. She remembered the simple quote she had read that morning, 'Choose the people who choose you'.

He asked her to join him for lunch. *What the hell*, she thought.

His loud voice didn't bother her this time. His world suddenly sounded intriguing and interesting. The Linking Road underbelly was actually more fascinating than some guy with daddy's money who worked in a boring factory and drove a fancy car, she thought to herself.

He told her about some business he was starting where he was importing some parts from Taiwan.

'Are you smuggling?' she asked in shock.

'No, not smuggling, just some money laundering,' he said.

She laughed out loud. *That line is going in my book*, she thought.

He had this beautiful childlike quality, he was excited about everything, even his semi-boring business ideas of importing steel parts from Turkey. He radiated positivity, and there was nothing jaded or cynical about him unlike the older guys with whom she crossed paths.

He touched her; his hands were rough with callouses. She glanced shyly at his hands. Rough, thick, big hands. She'd always been attracted to men with rough hands.

She told him stories about her last trip abroad, to Copenhagen. He told her stories about his last trip abroad, to Mecca. His family was very religious. He fasted on Eid. His sisters wore burkhas and had had arranged marriages.

He told her he wanted to be rich. She asked him what rich meant to him.

She told him that, to her, it meant leading a meaningful, purposeful life with love and friends and . . . He cut her short.

'Only rich people say that,' he said.

They laughed. He had a sense of humour.

'I'm not rich,' she said.

'I've only recently started earning enough to have savings again,' she said.

'You are rich,' he said.

'What's rich for you?' she asked.

'Rich is earning Rs 1,00,000 or more a month,' he said, 'you're in that 1 per cent of India.'

He worked five businesses, ran around all day but earned less than Rs 50,000 a month.

Her day was just sitting at her desk writing, editing or travelling. She told him about her space on Mount Mary Road, bright and beautiful with trees all around.

He told her he lived with six people in one house. She told him she lived alone.

He took her hand, looked in her eyes and asked if he could see her place . . .

She opened the door. He followed her inside.

They walked into the living room. She struggled with the lamp. He leaned in and helped her fix it.

'You need a man around the house,' he said, his eyes not leaving hers.

'No, I don't,' she said and laughed.

She went to the kitchen, poured him some coconut water. He followed her, took a sip, put it down, pulled her towards him and kissed her.

It wasn't a great kiss; he didn't even know how to kiss, but she liked it all the same. His cologne bothered her but she tried to ignore it. It wasn't good at all; he clearly wasn't skilled.

But they had a chemistry, an attraction. Maybe it had been too long since she had met someone.

What she liked about him was his quick wit; he was funny without fully knowing it. It felt good to be wanted again.

When he left, she wrote in her journal. 'He's like a blank canvas, just waiting for me to splash some colour and turn him into a masterpiece. He will be my little project. He has a lot of potential.'

The next day he came over, eager to see her again. He was rushing.

'You've never waited?' she asked?

'No,' he replied. He had never even heard of the concept of doing it for more than five minutes.

She laughed. What a patriarchal world he came from! 'What about the girls you've been with?' He said they seemed very happy. She raised her eyebrows in doubt.

'Well, I need more than five minutes,' she said. He kissed her and said he was a quick learner.

'And, when you meet me next time, don't wear cologne,' she said.

And this is how it began; she the teacher, he the student. Her sadness was gone, replaced by serotonin and all the love chemicals.

And as they lay there that night, her hair flowing all over his chest, he rubbing her back with his rough hands, he told her that he had never felt like this before. He had never felt this deep a connection.

She remembered reading a line somewhere: 'The magnets in your bones are drawn to the iron in my blood.' She whispered it in his ear. It seemed to go over his head.

He smiled at her, that big sincere smile. She closed her eyes, happy. His crooked nose didn't bother her anymore. He was sweet and nice. And that's what she needed right now.

He left at 5 a.m. His dad had been calling non-stop— fifteen times all night. She laughed it off.

Then she wrote a text to the Iranian guy with whom she was supposed to go on a date. 'I met someone. Sorry.'

She then copy-pasted the text and sent it to Mr Linking Road and went to sleep, smiling, happy.

The next day, she woke up, a smile on her face. With flashes of the night before, she sang softly to herself.

She reached for her phone, opened WhatsApp and saw many texts from Linking Road. 'Babe, this is too intense. You cut him off but I haven't decided what to do with the other people in my life. Are we cutting off our options without even discussing it?'

Wait, what? Linking Road has options?

He came over but this time to tell her he had other girls, booty calls, people he was dating. Plus there was a Dutch girl who was coming into town tomorrow to be with him for two months. They were going to the Magnetic Fields music festival together and had booked a tent.

She was confused. He was going to Magnetic Fields?

'You go to music festivals? I thought you were a simple guy from Linking Road who goes to Mecca for a holiday.'

'I like electronic dance music (EDM),' he said. 'I've been saving for two years to go to Magnetic Fields.'

'Why did you chase me for so long if there's a girl you're going to a music festival with?' she asked.

'I didn't think it would be this intense,' he said. 'I just thought we would be casual.'

'Wait, what? You wanted to be casual?'

'Yes,' he said. 'I thought we were just hooking up.'

'Don't you go to the mosque every Friday and fast for Ramzan?'

'So?' he said. 'Look, I don't have this connection with anybody, but I can't just ditch the Dutch girl. She knows nobody else in India.'

'I want to be in a monogamous relationship,' she said.

'That's a relationship,' he said. 'I am more inclined towards polyamorous casual type. Actually, I don't believe in relationships. I want to float.'

She sat there in shock. *Wait, who was he?* 'I thought you were a sweet guy who went to Hajj; someone who didn't know how to kiss till two days ago.'

'I also do acid and LSD sometimes,' he said. 'That's when I moved from being religious to liberal. Also, one day, in Bangalore, when I was at home, which was filled with religious books, my female friend came over drunk with another girl and they invited me into a threesome. Since then I've had four threesomes.'

She sat there staring at him.

Was she just bad at reading people?

'I think we should have a threesome,' he said.

'I am not attracted to women,' she said annoyed.

'No, with another man. I want to gift you that.' He started showing her pictures of his Brazilian neighbour.

'I'm not interested, thanks. That would be very awkward. I like one-on-one intimacy. And I want to be in a monogamous relationship.'

'This is harder for me than you but I am going to stop seeing you for a while. I can't dump the Dutch girl; I have too much guilt.' He walked to the door.

He turned and looked at her dramatically.

'I'm really attracted to you. And this is the best intimacy I've ever had. It's hard to leave. You're also the peak of my dating career,' he said.

'What?' she exploded. 'Dating career? Did you read that somewhere? What kind of ridiculous statement is that. You are really weird and immature.'

He left.

The next day, not a single text came from him. This was after a month of him texting every hour, every single day, starting from 'Good Morning'.

She was sad.

She opened Instagram and came across a meme.

It said, 'Men are like dogs who chase cars. When the car stops moving, the dog stops and wonders why it was chasing the car.'

She ate some chocolate.

'Could I be in a casual relationship?' she scribbled in her notes.

'It would be like settling for a big piece of chocolate cake with sugar when I am really craving for wholesome daal and chawal.'

She scribbled more, 'What is the charm of casual dating? Is it the freedom to explore different people without the pressure of commitment? Or is it a way to guard our hearts and avoid the vulnerability that comes with deeper emotional involvement?'

Her phone beeped. She looked at it. It was the attractive salt-and-pepper art collector she had spoken to at a farmer's café, asking if she wanted to go for a film. She said yes.

Her date went well with Salt and Pepper. He had a grounded energy. He was nice, a gentleman, thoughtful, kind, attractive. Maybe this could be something. A week went by; she saw Salt and Pepper a lot. They went to nice restaurants, they attended parties and chatted late into the night. She was attracted to him. But he had that older energy. His humour was rimmed with sarcasm, and when she didn't laugh, he told her she was killing his jokes. She missed the innocence, freshness, brightness and enthusiasm of Linking Road.

She missed his simplicity, excitement, eagerness and smile. Also he was quick and made her laugh without even knowing he was making a joke.

Why are guys my age so cynical? she thought to herself.

Her phone rang. Linking Road was calling. He came over, sugar-free chocolate mousse in hand. 'No sugar,' he said, beaming. She put it on the counter and took a bite. He took one too. He made a face and almost spat it out.

She wiped her face laughing.

'Why are you here?' she asked, even though she was happy to see him.

'I can't stop thinking of you,' he said. 'You're the most beautiful woman I've ever met.'

His mom called. He answered, *'Haan Maa, main niche hi hoon, bus paanch minute.'*

They kissed. He really didn't know how to kiss and his lips were dry and chapped but she liked him too much to care. His phone rang again. And then kept ringing. She threw his phone on the floor from under her.

When they finished, she slapped him on his butt and said, 'Go home, Daddy is calling non-stop.'

He left her home buttoning his shirt on the way down.

He texted, 'I am still afraid I can't give you all the things you're used to.'

'Intimacy and companionship are all I need from my man,' she texted back. 'Look at my home, I have everything I need. I can buy my own Louis Vuittons (plural) and summers in Europe,' she said proudly. Not that she ever had bought an expensive bag in her life but she was feeling good about her financial situation. Just eight months ago, she was flat broke. Her influencer career had really taken off and she was working with the country's best brands now.

She lay on her couch and took another bite of her sugar-free chocolate mousse and smiled.

He texted, 'This is the best connection I ever had in my life.'

She laughed. Her power was back.

They started seeing each other every day, smiling happily, enjoying one another's company. They would

go on rides on his broken bike
and eat at hole-in-the-wall street
hubs.

His phone always rang at the
end of the night.

'*Aya*, Mumma,' he would say
and leave.

New Years was approaching.
She suggested they go on a trip. They
decided to go for the Kerala Biennale.
She didn't mind paying for the hotels, she
didn't want to stay in cheap places. She
could afford it now.

They walked around looking at art, happy
and in love. It was a sweet, deep connection in
spite of all their differences. Who said couples need
to be the same age, come from the same background or
like the same things? He had never looked at art before.
She enjoyed teaching him. He enjoyed learning.

As she held his hand and they watched the sun go
down in Kochi, he whispered in her ear, 'Thank you.
That was my first sunset.'

'You've never watched a sunset before?' she
exclaimed.

'Nope,' he said. 'Nobody in my life ever watched
sunsets. It was not a thing.'

Wow! She couldn't imagine a life without sunsets.

On the flight back, she snuggled up next to him and
said something about him being her boyfriend. He moved
uncomfortably. 'Why are you so uncomfortable every
time I mention us being in a relationship?' she asked.

'I don't want to be in a relationship,' he stated solemnly looking at his palms.

'Okay, let's not label it then,' she said.

'I can be happy with keeping the labels just for my wardrobe,' she joked.

He got very stiff and serious.

'Mount Mary, I like you,' he said. 'But I just don't want to give up my sexual freedom. I want to be able to go into a bar, get drunk and leave with a woman.'

'What?' she exclaimed loudly. People on the plane started staring.

She whispered, 'You want to have sex with random women at a bar?'

'People do stupid things when they are drunk. What if I am drunk?' he said.

'Are you serious?' she gasped.

'I know I'm going to be travelling for my business. What if I meet someone attractive I may want to sleep with?'

'You mean you're ready to give me, us and this connection that we have, up for some random girl you may meet at a bar?' she blurted.

'You don't know men,' he said. 'I may have a 10 but if I get a 4 at a bar, I will still want to go with her. I've always wanted an open polyamorous relationship from the beginning,' he said.

'I guess I've not been listening,' she said quietly to herself, and then said loudly, 'But then why were you calling me every day? And what's with the texts every two hours?'

'I guess, I'm in love with you and I hate that,' he said.

She smiled. 'Me too,' she said happily. 'But I am happy about it.'

'Love is like a cockroach,' he exclaimed loudly.

'Scary like a cockroach?' she asked.

'Cockroaches are icky,' he said. 'Lions are scary.'

'So, you find love icky?' she said.

'Yes,' he exclaimed, shuddering. 'Gross!'

'I love love,' she said.

'Eww,' he said.

'As soon as I feel love I want to get it off me. Yeah, love is a cockroach. I don't want love. I don't want a relationship. I don't want to be responsible for another human.'

'You don't want a relationship but just want the perks of a relationship?' she asked.

He nodded. 'I guess. Let's end it.'

'WOW! Are you serious? You said I love you and let's end it in the same breath?'

He shrugged.

'Oh okay fine, I will never see you again,' she said, visibly hurt.

'I'm cool with that,' he said. 'I can detach easily. I have no deep sentiment. You are emotional,' he said. 'I don't have emotions. I am practical.'

'You like love.'

'I hate love. Love is disgusting,' he said loudly.

The air hostesses were coming around checking if everyone had fastened their seatbelts. The plane was landing.

'I don't want to hurt you,' he said. 'I don't want to lie either. This is my truth. I want to taste different women from different countries. I can't stop here.'

Even at this moment, she had to admire his honesty.

'So you value this "sexual freedom " more than you value a sense of belonging?'

'Yes,' he said. 'I want to float. I don't want to belong. I believe in speaking the truth no matter the consequences. I've read Jordan Peterson's book, *The 12 Steps to Life*, and I follow it religiously.'

She looked out of the window. The sun was setting.

'I like to dress casually and date seriously,' she said finally trying to make a joke.

'I guess casual relationships can be a little escape from the pressures and expectations of traditional relationships.'

'I understand your anxiety!'

She pointed to the sunset. He smiled.

'Thank you for the sunsets,' he said.

'Thank you for the honesty,' she said.

The plane was landing. It was a rough landing.

They went their separate ways.

She was sad.

He texted her two months later: 'I miss you.'

'And what are you going to do about that?' she replied.

'Nothing. I can live with the pain. But I can't live with love.'

'Still believe love is a cockroach?' she asked.

'Yes,' he said. 'But can I come over? I want to say something.'

She hesitated.

'Please,' he said.

Five minutes later, he rang the bell.

'I had sex with lots of women,' he said.

'How was it?' she asked.

'Medium to bad,' he stated. 'I was wrong. It's not about other women. It's about me not wanting a relationship. I don't want to build on anything with another person or make plans for the future. I am not ready to be married.'

'Married?' she exclaimed. 'Who's getting married?'

'I have this niggling feeling when I'm with someone or getting close. I want to meet you, hang out, enjoy our time but then I want to disappear. I start feeling extreme anxiety when I feel feelings. But I miss you. Let's try this again. Can we do casual without commitment?'

She took a minute to process this.

'We can try keeping it light. But monogamous light.'

'Okay,' he nodded.

So they started to meet 'lightly'.

He would call her at around 8 p.m., asking her what she was doing. She would say not much and he would come over. This happened every alternate day. And every Sunday, they worked out together and then went to her house for dinner.

One night as they were laughing about something, she exclaimed, 'I love you.'

He hesitated.

'I love you too,' he said quickly as if it were a bad word.

'Is everything okay?' she asked. 'Cockroach feeling?'

He nodded.

He never spent the night, not even once. She didn't mind. She liked sleeping by herself.

She had an assignment in the Maldives again. She took him. He had never seen any place this beautiful. He dived and swam in the ocean for the first time. She enjoyed being able to gift him all his 'first times'. They loved their ten beautiful days in the Maldives.

He smiled at her on the last day and said, 'Thank you for these ten days of bliss.' He held her hand tight but looked away. He was distracted.

'All okay?' she asked.

He nodded, looking slightly disturbed.

'Your belly is sticking out,' he said.

'Oh,' she said. 'The diet has to start when I'm back home.'

On the plane back as she snuggled up next to him, he moved away and said, 'We are a mismatch. My ex was better for me. She was more easy-going and you have way too much energy for me.'

'Okay,' she said. 'Are you trying to jeopardize us again? Is your anxiety kicking in?'

'You will be betraying yourself if you settle for this half relationship,' he said. 'I can't watch you betray yourself,' he said.

She looked in his eyes. He kissed her. That terrible kiss. He still hadn't learnt to kiss.

But she still felt something.

'The magnets in my bones are drawn to the iron in your blood,' he whispered. He held her tight. She smiled.

'What's with you and trying to break up on aeroplanes after beautiful trips?'

He pushed her away. 'I'm serious,' he said. 'This has to end.'

'What? Why can't we just relax and go with the flow?'

'What about my spiral?' he said.

'Let's figure it out,' she said.

'I love you,' he quickly said.

'Why do you always say I love you so fast?'

'Because it gives me anxiety,' he yelled.

The stewardess turned around.

'Sssh,' she said.

'It makes my heart beat faster,' he said, looking very stressed. 'I can't do this.'

Other passengers were turning around, looking at them curiously.

'I don't want to love anyone,' he yelled again. 'It's disgusting!'

People were staring.

'Let's break up.'

'Oh my God, what happened to you in your childhood?' she half joked.

He was quiet.

'How do you break up with someone you never even committed to?' she asked softly.

The plane landed.

His eyes had turned cold and distant.

'You like love,' he said. 'Love gives me anxiety. What makes you calm gives me anxiety. What makes me anxious makes you calm.'

She took a deep breath. 'We can figure it out if you love me and I love you.'

'Why do you love me?' he suddenly asked. 'I'm not special.'

'You are special,' she whispered, 'very special. You're unlike anyone I know. You're the most special person I know.' She smiled sweetly, her voice heavy with emotion.

His eyes brimmed with tears. 'You're way better than me,' he said. 'You are the peak of my dating career.'

She cringed. 'Don't say that.'

'I know you're the best I could do,' he said.

They were at the baggage counter. He picked up his bag.

'I've got to go, I'm going out to Anti-Social, meeting some friends.'

'Let's at least take a cab back together,' she said.

'No,' he said.

'But we spent ten beautiful days in the Maldives.'

'I may meet someone else tonight, and I may have sex with them. Even though you're a 10, I am a man. I may want to try a 5 or even a 2.'

'Stop with this rating system,' she yelled. 'I am more than a number.'

People were looking again.

'I feel I am with a greedy man at a buffet who wants to try every single dish only to realize that they are all mediocre.'

'Maybe,' he said. 'I am greedy.'

'I have to go,' he said.

'You're so uncomfortable with vulnerability,' she said as people flooded in and around the airport around them.

'Stop analysing me. It's done. We are done.'

'I chose you because you chose me,' she whispered.

'You're too emotional,' he said.

'You're acting in survival mode like an animal stuck in a cage,' she said.

'Perhaps I am, but I will have sex with someone else tonight because I don't want to be in a committed relationship.'

Her eyes teared up.

He looked at her and murmured 'Sorry' before leaving.

As she rode back home alone in a taxi, she thought to herself, with tears in her eyes, 'Could I have done anything differently?' She scribbled in her diary, 'Could I separate love and sex or will it always be interconnected for me?'

She searched commitment phobic on Google.

She read:

'A relationship with a commitment phobic is literally a "whirlwind" romance. It's intense, passionate and then all of a sudden it's over and you have no idea what happened.'

Google couldn't be more accurate.

She knew she could continue the cycle with him, because he would come back but he would always just leave her with a trail of confusion, pain and heartbreak. It was time to move forward.

She dialled a number and called for a sugar-free chocolate mousse. As she sat eating it on her couch, the answer to her question came to her.

No, she couldn't have done anything different.

A month later, a text popped up.

'Hi Mount Mary, I have a schedule now. Monday to Thursday, I am available for other women.

Friday, no woman (break). Saturday, 11 a.m. to Monday 11 a.m., I am booked temporarily. She didn't reply.'

He called. She hesitated but then picked up.

'She's a new entrant in my life, met her on Hinge but no strings attached. We are polygamous. She knows as soon as she leaves I'm with another woman. But the truth is I miss you. I miss your smile. She's a little too naive for me. And she's twenty-four. I have to teach her everything, advise her on everything.

'But she's completely okay with open relationships. Sometimes she and my other partners share a cab and go home together after a party.

'Nobody does monogamous relationships anymore in Mumbai. Monogamy is outdated,' he claimed.

'Can we meet? Come join us for boardgames. She will be there but she's not jealous. Or I can come over?'

No way! She had learnt her lesson. It was time to make space for the next chapter.

RECIPE

Sugar-free chocolate mousse

LESSON LEARNT

1. When someone tells you they do not want a relationship, believe them the first time. Don't try to change their mind.

2. You can't have a relationship if both people are not equally invested and rooting for it.

3. Casual dating can be like a little black dress that you can slip into whenever you're in the mood for some fun and excitement. It can be liberating and empowering until one of you starts 'catching feelings'.

4. She learnt to read the signs of an avoidant attachment style.

Here are some:

a. Isolation is easier than connection for them.

b. Avoidant people find faults in their partners when they are feeling too close for comfort. (Perhaps Humble was avoidant too.)

c. If you're seeing a person who has an avoidant attachment style, you will most probably feel needy at a certain point.

d. Avoidants can have feelings for their significant others (most times) but always put themselves first. They can be very selfish.

WHERE IS HE NOW?

His 'boring' businesses are flourishing and he is in the 'top 1 per cent' now.

They are friends but do not meet often.

She asked him recently, 'Is love still icky like a cockroach?'

He said, 'Not as bad as a cockroach. But it is like a pigeon.'

The 'new entrant' in his life is still around.

Three thank you's and a sorry:

1. She thanks him for getting her out of the darkness that she was in before he came along.

2. She thanks him for always being there to solve any work issue she had.

3. She thanks him for his honesty.

She is sorry that she took him seriously when he wanted her to take him casually.

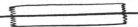

She misses:

1. His sharp mind, his quick wit and his problem-solving attitude.

2. His big smile and the twinkle in his eyes when he looked at her.

3. His hustle, and the excitement and pep in his step when he had a new boring business idea.

21

Passionate or Toxic, Is it Possible to have One without the Other?

He was the bad boy of Bollywood. He walked with a certain swag. With bulging biceps and toned calves, he was the poster boy of Gold's Gym. Girls swooned over him.

She had seen him over the years with a lot of women. She remembered being in a car with him and his then girlfriend and their common best friend twelve years ago. The actor and his girlfriend were almost having sex in front of her in the car. She was with Humble at that time, who barely touched her, and she remembered feeling a tinge of envy.

The way he was devouring her. *If only I had a passionate lover like that,* she had thought.

He was charming. He was hot. Not in the usual six-feet-three inches, broad-shouldered kind of way. More like five-feet-nine-inches sort of way. He was short, with smaller shoulders, but everything was nicely packaged. Like a perfect Ken doll.

He walked up to her twelve years later as she struggled with the 10-kg weights in her hands, sweat dripping from her forehead.

'Don't bend so much when you do dead lifts,' he said.

'All right,' she said.

'Nice tan,' he said to her.

'Oh, I just returned from Goa,' she said blushing. 'You're tanned too,' she mentioned, eyeing his popping tanned toned biceps.

'I've just come back from Fiji,' he mentioned.

'Wow. How was it?' she asked.

'Twelve girls and me,' he said.

There was a pause. She didn't know how to react.

'For a movie,' he said.

'Oh,' she laughed uncomfortably.

'Yeah, two of them were very into me. I tried a threesome too. But I liked a fourth one, shorter, but with bigger boobs. But when she saw me with these two she didn't want to have sex with me.'

'Oh,' she said, thinking *too much information.*

'I was getting over a break-up,' he said. 'My last girlfriend ended up being a hooker. You know, to rich Arab dudes in Dubai.'

'Oh,' she said, shocked.

'When I found out, I went to a party, grabbed the first girl there, took her to a room and just as my dick was about to enter her, I took a picture and sent it to my ex and said, "At least when I do it, I'm honest."'

'Oh my God,' she said, shocked. 'You took a picture of her private part and your dick?'

'Yes,' he said proudly.

'And the girl was okay with you taking the picture?'

'Yes,' he said, 'she's a good friend.'

She stared at him wide-eyed. 'That's a very good friend indeed.'

'Anyway,' he said, 'The Fiji threesome was good for me. I'm finally over the hooker. Would you like to go for dinner?' he asked her in the same breath.

'Er,' she looked at him for a minute. *One of India's most desirable men is asking me out for dinner. But that threesome talk and the photo of the sex and . . .*

'I'm sure you love sushi,' he said and flashed his beautiful symmetrical whitened teeth.

She blushed. He did have a nice smile. And, of course, who doesn't love sushi?

'I'll pick you up at 8. Izumi. I'm making a booking,' he said with a wink.

Oh well, why not. She was going through another dry phase and here was this hot celebrity Ken Doll trying to take her to dinner. Was she really going to say no?

Her aunt's voice echoed in her head, 'Beggars can't be choosers.'

'Sure,' she told him. 'I am NOT a beggar,' she replied firmly to her inner aunty thought.

He picked her up in a swanky new white Mercedes. He got out of the car to open the door and told her she looked beautiful. *A perfect gentleman.*

He self-parked his car. 'I don't like using valets for my expensive cars,' he said. 'This baby can only be driven by me.'

Inside the restaurant, she sighed in pleasure as the sushi melted in her mouth.

'This spicy salmon sushi is divine.'

'That's my plan,' he whispered. She loved his voice, deep and soft. *He was definitely sexy.*

'My plan is to get you to have a mouth orgasm first,' he said. 'And then, I will give you an orgasm down there.'

If any other man had said that she would have left but Ken Doll's voice was soft and deep, and she just fluttered her lashes.

He suddenly bent down, hiding under the table.

'Oh no.'

'What?' she asked, her sushi almost falling out of her mouth with his sudden movement.

Ashitosh Raheja passed by.

'He once threw cake in my face,' he exclaimed.

'What? Why?'

'A girl he liked was all over me.'

'Oh,' she commented.

'I wasn't even into her but she kept rubbing her tits on me.'

She nodded, not knowing how to react to this very unnecessary information.

'Even his bitch was licking my ankles and almost humping my leg,' he said.

She looked shocked.

'He's always been jealous. Even of his dog liking me more.'

'Oh,' she said relieved. 'You meant his dog.'

'Yeah,' he said. 'But it was a bitch.'

Ashitosh Raheja came over.

She got up, hugged him and said hi. The actor sheepishly got up from under the table. They shook hands.

Ashitosh left.

'Did you see that?' he exclaimed.

'What?'

'He gripped my hand really tight.'

She shook her head. 'Maybe you're imagining it,' she said.

'NO!' he exclaimed. His voice was getting louder.

'Men know. He probably wants to poke you. Unless you guys have already done it. Have you fucked him?'

'Er, no,' she said frowning.

'Men are so jealous,' he exclaimed. 'He definitely wants to poke you. Men hate on me all the time. When I walk into Gold's Gym with Arman and Sanjay, all the boys hate on us.'

He paused to see her reaction. She looked at him blankly.

'It's because all the girls drool when we enter.'

She nodded. 'You do have a nice body,' she said.

He flashed his smile. 'Thank you. You have a banging body too,' he said. 'You're so plump. Very child woman. Just like I like it. I love just a little plump, bordering on fat.'

She wasn't sure if she should be flattered or offended.

He leaned in. She could smell his cologne. He smelled rich, like the South Mumbai boys always did, of their fancy cars and their fancy US education. He kissed her.

This guy certainly did not waste any time and he was good.

A really good kisser indeed!

'I like you, dolphin,' he said. 'Can I call you dolphin?'

'Sure,' she said. 'I like it.'

'Or do you prefer boob-ae,' he asked.

'Dolphin, definitely dolphin,' she said. 'Can I call you Biceps?' she asked. 'You do have the best biceps I've ever seen.'

'Of course, Dolphin, you can call me whatever you like,' he said playfully.

'They left the restaurant holding hands. As they walked out, his expression changed in a matter of seconds—it went from smiling to fuming.

'What?' she asked.

'This mofo has parked his cab right in front of my Mercedes. How are we going to get out?'

Biceps walked up to the taxi and started yelling for the driver. The cab was empty. He asked the valets close by. They shrugged.

'Let's go back inside,' she said. 'We can wait it out. Have another drink maybe.'

'No,' he said firmly, looking very upset. 'This cab driver has to be around here. EHHHHH,' he started yelling in a hero style. '*Yeh gaadi ka* owner *kahan hain. Tum do* minute *main nahi aye toh main yeh* window *ko marega.* I will break this cab.'

She was embarrassed. She felt like she was in a movie, and he was the hero. Anti-hero more like it.

People were turning around and pointing. Someone came for a selfie with him.

'*Abhi nahi*,' he said, fuming.

He walked up to the cab and punched it. BAM!

She was shocked. Was he actually punching the empty cab?

'I am going to break this cab window,' he yelled and gave it one more hard punch.

Out of nowhere a man ran up, opened the cab and moved it.

'Next time you do something like this, I will break your face,' he shouted.

She was shaken. Wow, he was so angry . . . over a cab? His sexy soft whispery voice could get that loud and unsexy?

They sat in the Mercedes and drove in silence for five minutes. She felt very uncomfortable. Then he turned to her with a forced smile, 'Your place or mine?'

'Er,' she said. 'Can I just go home? I'm tired.'

'Really?'

'Yes, please,' she said.

'Oh,' he looked very disappointed. 'You don't have sex on the first date?' he asked in a charming way. His smile was back, his voice whispery and deep again.

She shook her head.

'But I do,' he said laughing.

She couldn't help but laugh. He was so cocky.

He stopped the car and kissed her.

Oh my God, he was such a good kisser. Probably all that experience.

'So,' he said, 'are you taking me home?'

'No,' she said firmly.

He dropped her home.

'I'm er, I . . . I'm a little shaken up after all that yelling,' she said as she opened the car door.

'But,' he said, 'if I didn't yell, we would still be there.'

'Maybe,' she said.

'No, definitely,' he said tight-lipped.

'Oh well, I wouldn't have minded another drink. Good night,' she said and slipped away.

He watched her walk away, looking very sad.

The next day when she woke up, there were five missed calls and five texts from Biceps.

The phone rang again.

'Please can we meet?' he begged. 'I'm really really sorry I scared you. Please forgive me. I like you, Dolphin. Not just for your plump body, which is pretty banging, but I have this feeling that we are connected from a past life. We are going to end up together in Goa, with a dog in a villa. I can see it.' They had similar backgrounds and common friends, belonged to the same generation, and he was so into her. She thought, '*Chalo*, why not? Let me give this a try.'

And that's how it started. Biceps was a very persuasive and attentive boyfriend. He found everything sexy about her—her unruly hair, her no make-up look, her protruding belly, the gap in her teeth.

And while girls drooled over him when they went out, he had eyes only for her. All the time! She was being 'love bombed'. In the best way! She enjoyed the attention and felt special and sexy. Nobody had ever been that into her.

He insisted on paying at restaurants, he picked her up from the airport, he called her every day.

Biceps drove all the way from Cuffe Parade to see her in Bandra every single day.

He was a good boyfriend. Correction: a great boyfriend.

But with that much passion also came that many insecurities.

If she didn't reply to a text immediately, he would get very upset. His whole mood would change.

'You didn't send me an emoji at the end of your text. Are you upset?' he asked.

'No, no,' she said. 'I was just busy.'

She realized that he just could not regulate his mood or control his temper. And he got triggered very easily.

Once they were at a party when someone casually said that *Kashmir Files* could be a propaganda film, paid for by the government. 'Have you watched it?' he yelled. 'You fake sheep, you're all pseudo intellectual liberals.'

She started having second thoughts about the relationship because of these sudden outbursts. This would in turn trigger his insecurities even more. 'You're second guessing us,' he would say. 'You are not giving me stability in this relationship.'

Once the two of them and his friend Rik were in Goa together. Rik was being extremely grumpy, so when he went to the bathroom she said jokingly, 'If Rik wants to go back to Bombay, don't discourage him.' He laughed so she took the joke one step further, 'You can even encourage him if you like.' She thought he would laugh but his face turned red. He started yelling in the restaurant. 'Rik is my friend since we were six.'

'Shh! Please don't create a scene,' she begged.

'You are so selfish asking me to ask him to leave,' his voice boomed. Everyone in the restaurant turned to look at them.

'This is the reason you have no close friends,' he said.

'That's not fair. Don't weaponize what I told you when I was vulnerable.'

'But it's true,' he continued, 'you don't have friends like I do. Your friends change every six months.'

She ran to the bathroom feeling ashamed, not wanting to create a bigger scene.

His temper always shocked her, his whispery sexy voice changing in a matter of seconds. And when she asked him to stop yelling, he would say, 'This is not yelling.'

She could tell his anger came from a place of insecurity, but it shook her up, and she would retreat and stonewall him for a few days. This would make him angrier. This started their cycle of on and off and up and down relationship that quickly became toxic for them both.

Biceps got angrier when he was drinking. Once they were at his friend's party. He was talking about how he was against polygamous relationships. She was not into polygamy either, and she had heard his opinion on this subject before. Plus he was drunk and everyone else was drunk, and they were all repeating themselves, so she stood up mid-conversation to go to the loo.

Biceps pulled her back aggressively. She fell back in the chair, her skirt flying up. She turned to him, 'That wasn't cool.'

'It's not cool for you to get up when I am talking,' he said, his tone raised again. The party stopped.

She whispered, 'You're drunk. Please don't make a scene.'

'Drunk,' he said. 'You want to see drunk? I will show you drunk,' he got up and went to the bar. She sighed and went to the loo. When she returned she saw that he was sitting on the terrace with a bottle of whiskey and drinking straight from it. He made eye contact with her and raised the bottle and smiled.

'You're a child,' she mumbled. 'A forty-year-old child!'

A girl complimented her about how she loved the Romance part of her Travel Romance and Smiles Vlog.

'It's more sex than romance,' he yelled from the bar.

She had a lump in her throat. She couldn't take it anymore. She knew how hard she had worked to be where she was today and this guy had no respect for what she did. She burst out crying in front of everyone.

She excused herself, grabbed her bag and ran out of the party. Three girls ran after her. So did he.

'I'm sorry, sorry,' he said. 'You're a flower. I'm a thorn. I don't know what's wrong with me. I feel you're going to leave me.'

'I am going to leave you,' she said.

'Sorry, sorry. I'm so insecure,' he had tears in his eyes. 'I love you so much. I can't live without you.' If only he could be less crazy?

'Can a man really go from an insecure hot mess to Mr Cool, calm and collected? Will he ever truly change his spots?' she scribbled in her diary.

And so the cycle began. They would be good for a day, madly in love, and then she would say something and he would get triggered.

'Baby, now for thirty minutes in the gym, no phone.'

Immediately he would get defensive. 'You're the one who has her phone on. Every time your mom calls, you answer. You should see yourself . . .' And the whole gym would turn around to look at them. He didn't care who saw him losing it. She would walk off and they would break up. A week later, they would get back together and have the best make-up with fireworks!

One day he took her to a party with all his friends. 'Meet Rishi, the only guy in school who got more chicks than me. All the big-tittied ones were mine though because he was more an ass guy. But now I have both,' he said winking at her.

She cringed, embarrassed.

Rishi said, '*CHUT*.' He laughed. 'Yeah yeah I am a *chut* because you are what you eat.'

All his friends laughed. She felt uncomfortable.

She took him to a corner and whispered, 'Baby, I don't like you objectifying me like that in front of all your friends. Makes me feel uncomfortable.'

'Objectifying? Oh my God, you won't let me be me. I am praising you. You want me to change my personality!' he started yelling. Everyone turned.

She sighed. *There they go again.*

She was in a relationship in which she doubted the sanity of her boyfriend and herself. He could just turn in a matter of seconds.

And it got worse. Whenever she disagreed with him, he took it personally, got really defensive and there would be a massive blow up.

She started feeling she was with a child who had temper tantrums.

They tried to break up a few times but they always got back together—with fireworks. There were fireworks like never before, but outside the bedroom, she felt her mental peace on an all-time low.

There were a lot of firsts for her.

She had never felt so desired, they had common friends and similar lifestyles. She loved the way he smelled, she liked looking at his handsome face, she loved the way he held her hand tightly. On paper they were perfect.

But this up and down was feeling very unhealthy.

31 January 2019

They had, as per their pattern, broken up.

She was quite unwell.

He found out and, without caring about catching whatever she had, came over immediately to take care of her. He massaged her head all night. He got her food and water. He was so caring.

The next day, when she was sleeping, he woke up and left the room. In her sleep, she mumbled, 'No Happy New Year?' It was 1 January.

He didn't reply. She dozed off again. Two hours later she woke up and went out, still quite sick. He was sitting there, angry and shivering.

'You should have woken up earlier. You should have taken care of me. I told you I was freezing. You don't care.'

'But I was sleeping,' she said. 'I didn't know you were feeling sick.'

He insisted she knew and still ignored him.

'All I want is a hug from you,' he said.

'I am calling the doc,' she said firmly.

'You're snapping at me when I am sick. I took care of you yesterday.'

His voice turned, 'You have no compassion. You are karmically fucked. You are warped. You're selfish. You're going to die alone and sick.'

She just stared at him in disbelief.

Then he started crying in self-pity.

'This is over. We can't stay together,' she told him.

'But we are both sick,' he yelled. 'I don't want to make my parents sick. Have you heard of Covid? It's happening in China. Maybe we both have it. We have to stay together for fourteen days.'

'It will be HELL,' she replied. 'I don't want to be in this relationship anymore.'

'You can't commit to anything,' he shouted, and then started sobbing like a baby. 'Everything sucks for me right now. I have no work, no girlfriend,' he wailed.

She rolled her eyes, this was too much! It was affecting her mental peace. She left the room.

She scribbled in her notes, 'I am losing respect for him. Can you love someone without respecting them?'

'I am sorry,' he said. 'I am so sorry.'

'This was *not* working.'

But they kept at it. Kept trying. She didn't want to leave the relationship. Maybe because she was tired of switching chapters, maybe because her identity was attached to being in a relationship, maybe it was the physical connection, maybe because she felt so desired here, maybe because it had become a drug and she was addicted to this on and off toxicity.

The fights got worse.

'I need someone more conservative. You're too out there. You pressed your tits against him when you hugged him.'

That day a new issue had come up.

'You haven't watched even one of my movies.'

'But I am not saying I won't watch. No movies have released since we started seeing each other. And you're playing a gigolo in your latest one, I don't want to watch you having sex with twenty girls in a movie.'

'You're just on a high horse because your career is going well.'

'Why are you taking my strength and turning it into your weakness?' she said to him.

'Aren't you happy for me?'

'Yes, I am, of course I am,' he said.

But she couldn't help wondering, 'Are today's men truly comfortable with a woman who is more successful than them or does it still emasculate them?'

She wondered, 'Is it even possible to have a great career and a great relationship?'

He walked up behind her and held her waist. He massaged her shoulders.

That night, she scribbled in her notes 'Is fighting just a form of our foreplay? Are we fighting just to kiss and make up?'

They were in Pondicherry for a holiday. He went for a shower. He asked her to call for a towel. She forgot and got busy on her phone, editing her videos. He came out and saw her sitting on the phone and started packing his bags.

'OMG so sorry. I forgot about the towel,' she said running to the phone to call for a towel.

'You're selfish. You only think of yourself. I had to dry myself with a hand towel.'

'Sorry, sorry my bad,' she said.

It was midnight but he continued to book another hotel.

'You're not nurturing. I need someone nurturing. You're too much into your work,' he yelled. 'You just think you're so good because you're doing well in your career.'

She stopped, 'I want to enjoy my success. I do NOT want to apologize for it.'

'And baby I work hard at it. While you take your naps, I am on my laptop.'

'I am leaving,' he declared as he zipped his bag. 'I am so done with you!'

'Okay,' she sighed giving up.

He put his bags down. 'I love you.'

She looked away.

'You're abandoning me?' he asked.

'No,' she replied.

'You were ready to leave two minutes ago and abandon me,' she said.

This had to end—the break-ups, the passionate make-ups, the yelling, the crying, there was so much drama.

They had as many climaxes out of bed as they had in bed.

They were asleep. He woke her up.

'You're snoring,' he said.

'I am sorry,' she said in her sleep. 'Can you move up a bit?'

He jumped up, turned on the light and started measuring the bed. 'You pushed me,' he yelled.

'You're three times my size,' she said sleepily. 'How can I push you?'

'Look at the space you have, look at the space I have,' he raised his voice.

'Please lower your volume. How would you feel if I yelled at you all the time?' she asked him, also raising her voice.

'You think this is yelling,' he asked? 'Let me show you yelling.'

And then he started screaming on the top of his voice. The whole hotel must be awake now. She shut her ears. All she could hear him say was, 'I AM DONE WITH YOU, YOU'RE A C . . T.'

She couldn't believe it. He had crossed all boundaries now. He was abusing her, that too in English!

And, really, what was he getting hysterical about? Her asking for some space in bed? Even if she had more space, so what?

He stormed out of the room. She rolled around unhappily. In a relationship, when do you know that enough is enough? She went back to sleep.

He came back. 'I am not paying 10,000 a night to sleep in the balcony,' he exclaimed.

'I didn't ask you to sleep outside,' she said.

The next morning he tried to have sex with her. 'Are you apologizing for last night?' she said.

'No, this is just break-up sex,' he said harshly. She turned away.

'Enough,' she said. 'I can't!' She was crying. 'I need my peace back. And I have a big film coming up, I don't want to be so upset all the time,' she said.

'Film?' he said, surprised. 'You're acting?'

'Yes,' she said.

'But you didn't tell me you were going to act,' he said looking very shocked.

'What do you mean? I am an actor,' she said equally surprised.

'You're a blogger,' he said.

'I've been an actor since I was sixteen!'

'You're a retired actor. I didn't start dating an actor. I started dating a blogger,' he said loudly.

She stared at him, her eyes wide.

'It's a deal breaker. I don't want my future wife to be an actor and do intimate scenes on screen,' he said emphatically.

'But you are an actor!' she exclaimed in shock. 'Your brother is an actor. And you do movies where you're smooching all the women left right and centre. You're called the serial kisser of Bollywood.'

He started yelling, 'But you knew that since the beginning. You're suddenly changing your profession on me.'

She held her head in frustration, not knowing what to say. 'I have changed five professions till date; do I need to take your permission for that?'

He ignored her question and whispered, 'If you don't want me to do intimate scenes, I will stop. If it's a really big film, I will tell you and we can discuss it.'

'I will never stop you from doing something that is important to you. And seriously, you would not do a big show because I say don't do it?' she replied.

He started yelling again, 'Are you deaf? I just said I will not do it if it upsets you.'

She whispered, 'This is a really big show.'

'I can't see you kissing another man,' he said pleading. 'You have to choose. Acting or me.'

'I choose the show,' she said softly. 'I don't react well to ultimatums.'

'You have this burning desire to be an actor all of a sudden. You're choosing your career over me? This is what they call toxic feminism,' he said in tears.

'I will resent you if I give it up,' she said.

He was pacing up and down the room in anger, 'So go bloody do it,' he yelled.

'My career has been with me since I was sixteen. Men have come and gone. Nobody but me pays for my lifestyle. It's always been just me. Even this hotel. We are splitting it,' she said.

'Get off your high horse. You're a joke. You're pathetic. You want to stay in expensive hotels and have this lifestyle, that is too much for me.'

'Am I asking you to pay for me?'

'You don't know the L of love. There are more important things in life than movies and making stupid videos.'

'I'm leaving,' she said.

'But you promised we would be together forever,' he said.

'I promised to be together as long as it was a healthy choice for me,' she said.

He texted her when they were back in Mumbai.

'I am sorry, baby. I am so insecure but I love you. I can't see you kissing anyone else, even on screen. If you want to do it, okay. I will swallow it. Meet me? Let's figure it out?'

She didn't reply. It took all of her willpower to stay away. He had become her drug but she knew she just had to stay away or she would lose her mind.

RECIPE

Spicy salmon sushi

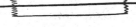

LESSON LEARNT

1. Toxic relationships are addictions.
They are not love.

Here's how it works:

1. Oxytocin when bonding cuddling and sex.

2. Dopamine when getting affection and attention.

3. Adrenaline when we are unsure if we will get the dopamine hit and

4. Cortisol during conflict.

The cocktail of these hormones is highly addictive!

And even though the relationship is full of conflict, we become addicted to the cycle and crave the highs of Dopamine and Oxytocin.

We live in false hope that our partner will CHANGE and the HIGHS will be consistent.

2. Long-term relationships are NOT built on great chemistry and hormones; they are built on great communication and creating a safe place to be our authentic selves.

3. Without communication and understanding even the HOTTEST relationships can run COLD.

4. If both partners are always fighting to be right, the relationship is wrong.

5. Relationships need work but it's important to recognize when a relationship feels more like work and less like joy.

6. Some people have a histrionic personality. It makes them dramatic, excitable, erratic and volatile.

But it also makes them sexy, flirtatious, seductive and charming.

She learnt she is not compatible with this type of personality.

7. She had already learnt to recognize the signs of a toxic relationship in chapter 18.

But she obviously didn't remember them.

This brings her to the conclusion that we repeat our patterns until we learn our lessons.

8. She needs a partner who is doing well on his own and doesn't feel threatened by her success.

9. Toxic relationships are like feasting on a mouth-watering meal that leaves you feeling bloated, drained, gassy. They drain your energy, dampen your spirit and stifle your growth.

WHERE IS HE NOW?

In therapy, she hopes.
If only he could calm down, maybe they could
give it another chance. Really? Had she not
learnt her lesson?

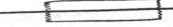

THREE THANK YOU'S AND A SORRY:

1. *She thanks him for his complete devotion to their relationship.*

2. *She thanks him for always making her feel like the sexiest woman in the world.*

3. *She thanks him for motivating her in the gym.*

She is sorry she second guessed this relationship right from the start and is equally to blame for making it toxic for disappearing for days after a conflict to come back again later for the Oxytocin high.

SHE MISSES:

1. The way he held the back of her neck when he kissed her.

2. His soft deep sexy bass voice (when he was not angry).

3. The way he looked deep into her eyes and held her hand tight!

22

ARE OUR PAST LESSONS
A BLESSING OR A CURSE?

14 February 2020

She scribbled in her notes, 'In Mumbai city, you are always looking for one of these three things— an auto, an apartment and a boyfriend. Today is Valentine's Day and I am determined to find a boyfriend.'

She opened Bumble.

She saw a profile of a tall guy, kicking a ball. She swiped right. It was a match! 'Are you really forty-one?' she asked.

He had a sweet young face.

'I'm thirty-one,' he replied. 'Sorry, किसी कारणवश मैं ऐप में अपनी उम्र नहीं बदल सक रहा हूँ। But I love older women. They are so much HOTTER! मेरी उम्र की लड़कियों के साथ मेरे पास बात करने के लिए कुछ नहीं है।'

She sighed. Here's another boy with the MILF fantasy.

'I've just got to accept the fact that forty-year-old men are looking for thirty-year-old women? And thirty-year-old men are looking for forty-year-old women?' she scribbled in her notes.

'Besides, when was the last time I found a forty-year-old man hot?' The ones she did like—Biceps and Salt and Pepper—had turned out too angry and cynical.

If unmarried men can be Players, unmarried women can be MILFs.

'Tell me more,' she wrote and continued swiping.

He replied a minute later.

'Hello, I would love to get to know you.'

'Skip the texts and get on a video call?' she typed back.

'Yes,' he replied.

The very next minute her phone buzzed. It was always uncomfortable to pick up and talk to a stranger. But hey, this was modern-day romance. You had to swallow the discomfort if you wanted to meet someone.

A very sweet face with an unruly beard said hello shyly.

Of course, it was uncomfortable for him too.

'Hi,' she said. His house walls were yellow, he was lying down.

'I have to admit something,' he said. '*Main* Faridabad *mein rehta hoon.* I was in Mumbai yesterday so maybe that's how *humne match kar diya.*'

'Sorry, *mera* English *fluent nahi hain.*'

'No problem,' she said.

'I work for a sports company,' he said. 'I organize marathons. We are arranging one in Mumbai, so I will be back there.'

'How did you get into marathons?' she asked.

'I used to be a pro footballer. *Maine* India *ke liye bhi khela hai, par* then I hurt my back.'

'Okay,' she said. 'I make travel videos.'

'I live to travel,' he said, smiling. He had a very nice smile and a very expressive sweet face. She couldn't see his body but his height on Bumble was six feet three inches.

English wasn't his first language but so what? She had dated a Brazilian guy who spoke less English than him.

'*Agley mahine main* Mumbai *mein hoon,*' he said. 'Can we meet?'

'All right,' she replied.

On 20 March 2020, she got a message.

'Hi, *main* Mumbai *mein hoon.* Can we meet?'

'Sure,' she said. 'Why not? Hope you're safe?' she asked.

'I hope you're safe,' he replied. She laughed.

Covid conversations had taken over the world and everyone was scared. *What was happening to the world?*

She sent him the address to a beautiful rooftop restaurant at Soho House, which was a members-only club, and left his name at the reception.

It was a Sunday. She sat by the poolside in a cabana and waited for him. Her phone beeped.

'Sorry, the traffic is crazy. I'm going to miss the sunset. I'm stuck at Juhu beach, I can see it from the cab.'

'All right,' she replied. *The poor guy was coming from Navi Mumbai or Virar or somewhere far,* she thought.

After thirty minutes, a very tall man with a very unruly beard walked towards her. His jeans were tight and up to his waist, and he had a checked shirt on.

'Oh my God,' she mumbled to herself.

Well, this is whom I am going to have dinner with tonight, and I'm going to make the most of it, she thought.

She did a quick makeover reel in her head. That beard could go, the jeans could be replaced with ankle length pants and his shirt could be a white tee to compliment his tanned skin and show off his biceps. He immediately looked much cuter to her. She smiled.

He smiled. He had a sweet infectious smile. Perfect teeth. And he was tall. Almost too tall.

'Are you really just six feet three inches?' she asked.

'Maybe an inch taller,' he said.

He sat down. The music was loud. He said something, but she couldn't hear him.

'*Jagah mast hain*,' he repeated.

'Yes, it is,' she replied.

They leaned back, watching the people as they swayed to the music. The sky went from orange to purple to black.

They both couldn't really hear each other, as they tried to make conversation. She was thankful for the loud music.

'Do you want a drink?' she asked.

'Yes. A beer, please.'

She ordered a glass of red wine for herself.

It was nice to just sit back and enjoy watching all the fashionable people walk back and forth. The drinks loosened them up a bit and helped them feel more comfortable.

They ordered dinner. And then laughed at how terrible the dish they had ordered was.

Foam and some sugar syrup.

'*Mere liye toh bahut hi* fancy *hain*,' he said. 'I'm more a paratha and dahi kinda guy.'

'Haryana's staple diet,' she said laughing. 'But how do you Haryanvi men get so tall and well-built just eating that?'

'Thank you, Mummy, Daddy,' he said. She laughed.

They went to the other side of the terrace to check out the planes that were landing and taking off from the airport.

He checked his phone. 'Country *shayad* lockdown *main jayega* from tomorrow,' he said.

'Yes,' she replied. 'Do you think that's even possible? How can they shut down everything? I can't believe it,' she said. 'I mean, this is India, people need to eat.'

'I will take a flight home tomorrow,' he said. 'I don't want to be stuck in Mumbai.'

'Is that so bad? We could eat more fancy food,' she flirted.

'I will eat that for you if you insist,' he replied shyly.

'Do you have green eyes?' she asked him, suddenly noticing the colour of his eyes.

'I think so, people say that,' he said. 'I don't know what colour they are.'

'You don't know how tall you are? You don't know the colour of your eyes?' she said.

'I know the colour of your eyes,' he said. She smiled.

'You have a nice face,' she said. 'Very symmetrical. Aquiline nose.'

'Aquiline, *woh kya hain*, Mohtarma?' he asked.

'Straight, not bent or anything,' she said with a laugh. 'Did you call me Mohtarma?' she said after a moment.

'Yes, you're a mohtarma. A lady.'

'Wow, that's a first! I can't wait to tell my friends.'

He laughed shyly and brought his lips closer to hers. She felt a current of electricity.

'I want to eat some parathas,' he said. '*Kahin aur jate hain?*'

'It's late. Not sure if anything will be open.'

'Let's go, I'm hungry,' he said. 'I need to feed my tall body.'

The server brought them the bill. She took it, opened her wallet. *It's probably too expensive for him*, she thought.

She paid. He didn't flinch or say anything They walked down.

'Let's go to Juhu beach for a walk,' she said.

'Yes,' he agreed.

It was very windy and silent on the beach. Suddenly it was just the two of them. There was no music to distract them from their awkwardness.

They walked towards the water. The stars were shining down at them and it was a full moon night.

He kept looking at her, staring at her mouth. She could feel he wanted to kiss her. But he definitely didn't have the guts.

If the country is going into lockdown tomorrow, I am going to be reckless tonight, she thought. He stared at her lips again.

The water touched her feet.

'Oh no,' she screamed, jumped and held his hand. He immediately held it back, quite tight, not ready to let it go.

The wind blew her hair in her face. He moved it with his other hand. She stood on her toes and kissed him.

He immediately kissed her back, holding on to her tightly. They stood there on the beach, the boy from Haryana and the girl from Bandra. They kissed for fifteen minutes and then he just picked her up and they continued to make out. And then, out of nowhere, he touched her butt.

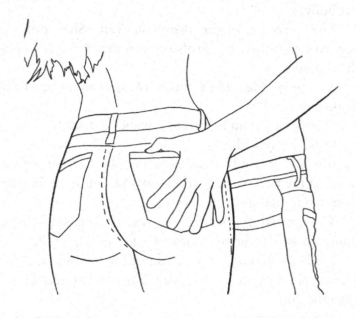

'Oh,' she exclaimed. 'Maybe too soon.'
    'Oh,' he said. 'Sorry!'
    'Do you really want parathas right now?' she asked.
    'I am hungry,' he replied.
    'Nothing will be open now,' she said.
    He looked down sadly.
    'Okay, let's go to my house and order or we could eat the food in my fridge.'

'Great idea,' he said softly.

So they took a rickshaw back to her place and kissed the whole way there.

As soon as they got into the house, he picked her up and carried her in, his lips pressed against hers.

'Do you still want to eat?' she asked.

'I want to eat you up,' he replied.

She hesitated for a moment.

He immediately stopped.

'Are you sure you want to do this?' he asked, his voice deep and sexy.

'Let's go slow?' she whispered.

He nodded.

They made out all night and fell asleep in each other's arms.

She woke up with a start ten minutes later with his loud snoring. Rrrhhhh! 'OMG, you must be kidding me,' she mumbled. She looked at his face in the dark. God, that beard was atrocious. What was she thinking? She took her pillows and crept out of the room and went to sleep on the sofa.

The next morning, she woke up first and went back to the bedroom. He was still snoring loudly.

She went to the balcony with her cup of green tea. She checked the news. Modi was going to address the country that evening.

Suddenly he came up from behind and hugged her.

'Hi!'

He was booking his ticket. '*Main flight book kar raha hoon.* Or I will be locked down with you.'

She giggled nervously. 'That could go either way for us,' she said.

'I should go,' he said. 'I want to be in Delhi if my parents need me.'

'Okay,' she said.

He booked his flight. 'I will have to leave for the airport in an hour,' he said.

'Don't you have any luggage?'

'Nope,' he said, 'just that backpack. Come on, let's play some football, I can teach you some moves.'

'I don't have a ball.'

He excused himself and came back a minute later with some toilet paper. He started dribbling it on his knees and feet and then he popped it at her. She caught it. An hour went by as if it were five minutes with them giggling and kissing and dribbling the toilet paper.

He then put on a Prateek Kuhad song, and they sang it together.

'It's time for me to go,' he said.

'Okay,' she said sadly, nervous about spending the lockdown alone.

She jumped up on him.

He held her and kissed her affectionately.

'I like you,' he said.

'Me too,' she said.

'Okay. Bye, Mohtarma,' he said.

And with that he turned around and left.

She laughed but tears rolled down her cheeks. She was emotional because of this whole lockdown thing.

PM Modi announced the lockdown that night. She spent the night restless, not knowing what was going to happen next. Will her parents be okay on their own? How will she live all alone? How long will this last? Her head was buzzing with questions.

He called her the next day from Delhi. He was at his friend's home. He didn't want to risk going to his parents' after the flight.

She told him she was feeling anxious.

'*Main hoon na*,' he said.

She smiled. He had this really nice calming energy.

And so, what she thought was the end of a one-night stand was actually just the beginning of a long-distance lockdown love affair.

They spoke every day. He sent her songs. He calmed down her anxiety about the lockdown.

They worked out together on video calls.

He taught her how to cook gobi parathas. He watched patiently on video calls as she burned a couple of parathas, finally very excited when she got it right.

It was as if they were living together but in different apartments.

She had a virtual lockdown lover.

One day, he got a letter from his office terminating his contract.

'I'm jobless,' he said to her with a laugh. 'They let go of my entire department. They didn't even pay my last month's salary.'

They discussed his job options. He was so calm. He wasn't overly upset or rushing into getting another job.

'*Jo hoga, so hoga*,' he said with a smile.

'Do you have savings?' she asked.

'No,' he said laughing. 'My salary was 50,000. What can I save with that?'

She nodded.

The boy from Haryana and the girl from Bandra were talking every day, five times a day. He spoke Hindi, she replied in English. They watched shows together virtually. They sang karaoke together. They talked about how they would go to Kashmir together after the country opened up. They were each other's corner through all the phases of the lockdown.

'I want to live in a home with lots of trees around,' she said.

'Me too,' he replied.

'In Goa?' she asked.

'Yes,' he said.

Haryana and Bandra dreamed of a life together after lockdown.

They exchanged music on Spotify. They sent each other memes. He taught her how to make kadhi pakora.

One day, she suggested he shaved his beard off. And so, she sat there on the phone while the beard came off.

'Wow, you actually have a nice sharp jaw hidden under that bush,' she exclaimed.

He smiled, his dimples more prominent now.

'What if it was a double chin?'

'I was worried about that,' she admitted laughing. 'But I love your calming energy. We could be friends,' she teased.

He really had a cute face, and she loved the fact that he didn't even know it or cared.

She noticed how even-tempered he was. He didn't seem to get upset at all about anything. Even when the country kept extending the lockdown he was all right. She would freak out but he would calmly console her even though he was the one who had no savings or a job. 'I don't know how you are thirty-one and so mature, calm and chill,' she said to him. 'You really have zero anxiety. I've never seen that in anyone!'

He shrugged.

'I wish I could be this calm,' she said.

He was smart too. He read a lot and had trivia about everything. She called him her encyclopedia. He had EQ and IQ.

He told her about how his mom worked on a farm in Haryana, milking cows, and how his father had a government job earning Rs 5000 a month.

But they still put him and his brother in good schools and gave them the best education.

'My brother is a doctor,' he said proudly.

'That's so incredible,' she said. 'Your parents must be so proud.'

'They worked very hard for us,' he said.

'What about you?' she said. 'What do you want to do with your life?' she asked him. 'You're so smart. What would you do if you could do anything?'

He shrugged.

'*Main jahan hoon, vahan khush hoon. Itna bojh kyon leneka.*'

'You have NO AMBITIONS?' she asked.

'I had once, I wanted to play football for India. But now, after the injury, I can't. I am okay. Happy to do minimum work and maximum chill,' he said laughing.

She nodded, not laughing.

'*Kya hua,*' he said noticing her pensiveness.

'Just wondering how you're so chill with no job, no savings, no plan,' she said.

'You care a lot about money,' he said.

'No,' she replied. 'Not money. More about passions, ambition, and I like being productive.'

'Productive *se kya hoga?*' he said.

'I guess,' she said. 'I don't know. You do have a point. I've always been ambitious. Want to accomplish things. And I like earning well too. Makes me feel confident.'

'Work is your identity?' he said.

'What is yours?' she asked.

'I am a good person, I am honest. This is my identity. What does all this productivity give you?' he asked.

'I guess it keeps me occupied and excited about life,' she replied. 'Plus it gives me money.'

'What does money give you?' he said.

'Freedom,' she replied. 'Money buys me freedom. To do what I want, go where I want.'

'To pay for that fancy food at Soho House,' he teased.

She laughed. 'Yes,' she said, 'when it opens I will eat a lot of bland fancy food.'

'*Mujhe zyada bojh nahi lena hain*. I have a house. I have food. *Bas*, I'm happy. I do not like that fancy food, I am okay with my gobi paratha.'

'But,' she replied, 'you live with your parents. Don't you want your own place someday?'

'I love my parents,' he replied.

'In Goa? With trees around us.'

'You will buy that house,' he said.

She raised her eyebrow.

'I will come live with you. *Main toh chill karunga*,' he said jokingly.

But was he really joking? Every joke has some amount of truth in it to be funny. But this wasn't feeling funny anymore.

That night, she thought about their conversation. He was so different from everyone she had met.

So content.

Was being content a blessing? Or a curse?

She wished she had a little of that groundedness and *theherav* as he called it.

She had so much restless energy about being productive.

But that's what makes me successful, she thought.

March went into April, went into May. She was getting very restless, alone at home.

They had been speaking for hours every day since March.

. She was very impatient now. 'I'm bored just being on the phone all day,' she announced.

Phase 2 of the relationship came sooner on the phone without the distraction of the physical connection.

In the beginning, his incorrect English didn't bother her. Nor did the fact that he said the same thing in five different ways, but as time passed, she started noticing these little things.

It's so true. All the things you fall in love with in Phase 1 of the relationship start bothering you in Phase 2.

She started questioning his lack of ambition now.

'But how can you be so content?'

'I am happy,' he would reply.

She started being a bit snappy with him and correcting his English, but instead of being mad at her, he thanked her for improving his English. He even enrolled in online English classes.

'I'm going to make sure I can speak English for you,' he said.

'Lockdown will open soon. Let's plan Kashmir,' she exclaimed.

'I have something to tell you,' he said sadly. 'Sorry it's bad news but I can't afford it. It's been a few months since I lost my job and I have no savings.'

'Of course,' she said. 'I understand.'

They were quiet.

'But then how do we see each other?' she asked. 'Lockdown will end soon. I'm dying to go somewhere. I can't come to Faridabad; you live with your parents.'

'Yes,' he replied quietly.

'So, you can come here?' she said.

'I don't have money for a ticket,' he said.

Both of them were quiet.

'But you said, we would travel after the lockdown.'

'One can dream,' he said.

'I could buy you the ticket,' she exclaimed, 'but I don't want to be home once it opens. I am so sick of being in my house for so many months alone. I want to go somewhere. Let's go to Goa?'

'I would love to come but I have no money.'

'At all?' she asked.

'The little I have I want to save for a rainy day.'

'But this is a rainy day,' she exclaimed.

'No it is not,' he said.

There was a pause.

'I can buy you the ticket,' she said.

'Can you pay for the whole trip?' he asked.

She nodded.

'*Toh fir* I can come,' he said. 'Or I can come and just live with you when you come back,' he said. '*Vaise* I don't have a job.'

'You will move in with me?' she asked.

'Yes,' he said.

'In Mumbai?' she said.

He smiled. 'Yes.'

'And work?'

'*Dekh loonga*,' he replied. 'Maybe I can work for you,' he said. 'I like travelling.'

'But,' she said. 'That will be so weird. I will be your boss.'

He laughed. 'I like a sexy boss.'

She was quiet. She scribbled in her diary, 'I don't mind paying, I just want him to have some shame about it.'

She scribbled more, 'Could I be a sugar mama? On the one hand, it sounds like stepping into a role of power and independence. But on the other hand, I question whether it might create an imbalance in the relationship?

'But what if he pulls his weight by helping me with my work and fixing the house, making lunch? In the end would it be an equal relationship or would I struggle to respect him?

'Am I still stuck in the traditional roles of a relationship? Haven't I progressed?'

She couldn't keep her doubts from creeping in. Faridabad and Pali Hill were cute on the phone but was this realistic? She scribbled in her diary, 'And what about the societal judgments and stereotypes that come with being a sugar mama? Would I be able to practise the subtle art of not giving a fuck in this case?'

She wondered, 'How many people out there have a great chemistry with people they are embarrassed to introduce to their friends?'

Could she really have a relationship with this guy once lockdown was over? Or was she just lonely?

They started speaking less and less on the phone.

She started scrolling Bumble again. Another tall man looked at her from her screen, said he was a surgeon. She swiped right.

'Are you really a surgeon?' she wrote.

'Haha, I get that a lot,' he replied.

'Must be the muscles rippling under your t-shirt,' she flirted.

That night, when Mr Haryana called, she told him that she was done having a phone boyfriend.

'I want to start dating other people. And I want an equal. I don't want to be your sugar mama.'

She saw his beautiful green eyes fill with tears.

He took a deep breath. 'I understand,' he said.

'Can we still just be friends?' he asked.

'Of course,' she said tearing up too.

'This is not the end of us,' he said. 'I have learnt a lot from you.'

She smiled. '*Angrezi?*'

'Not English,' he said. 'Other things. To be ambitious. To have goals. To think bigger than I do.'

'So, will you?' she asked hopefully.

'I don't know,' he said. 'It's not in my nature. But I will try.'

She nodded, tearing up.

'How is this realistic?' she asked.

'I don't want to see you cry,' he said in a solemn, deep voice.

'I am happy to have you in my life in any way. Even as a friend,' he said.

He was so sweet.

Should she just let him come live with her? Work with her? She had made this mistake before with Black Don't Crack and the Israeli.

No, she had to learn from her past recipes.

She scribbled in her diary, 'Are my past lessons a blessing or a curse? Are they ghosts that haunt my present or are they giving me wings to fly?'

She spoke to some friends.

Her friend Malika said, 'First you pay for them and then they resent you for paying for them. Don't make the mistake I made.'

Her friend JJ warned, 'Don't do it again, you've done it before. Please now, don't be a fool again.'

She nodded.

She didn't want a sugar daddy but she didn't want to be a sugar mommy either.

He needed to find his path, on his own.

'Maybe this story isn't over yet,' he said to her on video-call, his eyes brimming with tears.

'Maybe,' she said.

They both were crying now.

'I guess this is what they call conscious uncoupling,' she said.

'*Voh kya hain?*' he said.

'A fancy way of breaking up,' she replied.

They laughed through their tears.

'We have love, but we don't have a path,' he said. 'And if we stay together, we will spoil what we have.'

She nodded.

They hung up.

She cried.

Break-ups are hard because we hold on to what it could have been. She scribbled in her notes, 'He could have been perfect BUT . . .

Will there ever not be a BUT?

Am I making the right choice?

Does anyone ever know if they are making the right choice or is it always a leap of faith?'

RECIPE

Gobi parathas

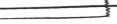

LESSON LEARNT

1. As unromantic as it sounds, compatible financial values are a very important question to consider.

2. If being a sugar mama makes you feel alive, confident and in control, go ahead and own it. Life's too short to deny yourself pleasure to explore unconventional relationships. But if it makes you lose respect for the guy or feel taken for granted, then you need to accept that.

3. Just as you would ask about someone's favourite dish or preferred cuisine, ask about their financial mindset and beliefs.

WHERE IS HE NOW?

*He still sends her memes and news articles. He
has a job with a digital media agency which he
doesn't love. He has a girlfriend whom he refuses to
speak about.*
*They meet when she visits Delhi; they still have love
and chemistry but don't act on it.*

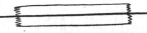

THREE THANK YOU'S AND A SORRY:

*1. She thanks him for keeping her somewhat
sane during the lockdown.*

*2. She thanks him for showing her that she
needs someone calm and centred.*

*3. She thanks him for showing her she
needs to find theherav in herself.*

*She's sorry she went with her head and not
her heart.*

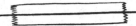

SHE MISSES:

1. His calmness and theherav (of course) and how he always had a solution for every challenge that she felt anxious about.

2. His big sweet smile and carefree attitude.

3. Learning about what was happening in the news and current affairs from him.

EPILOGUE

Where is she now?

She's turning this book into a very successful show on Netflix or Amazon Prime.

Meanwhile, she's still writing new chapters while scribbling questions in her notes. *In Nothing but Lipstick and Lingerie* is the working title of her next book.

Some of the next book chapters look like this:

Are all single people looking for a partner and all married people looking for freedom?

Are some people just luckier in love or do they work harder in relationships?

Is it possible to find a real relationship in Mumbai?

In the world of dating apps, can too much choice be just as dangerous as too little?

Will we ever truly know our partners or will there always be some secret?

Beyoncé got cheated on, Halle Berry got cheated on, Jenifer Lopez got cheated on, Salma Hayek got cheated on. Is it fair to assume everyone gets cheated on?

Could you cheat on someone you loved? Or does love have nothing to do with it?

Are the non-negotiables negotiable?

Do we need to keep our finances separate in relationships? Do separate bank accounts mean less conflict?

In this modern world, what's the ratio men and women should pay? Is 70/30 fair? Or 50/50?

Would you rather have freedom but pay for everything yourself or live in a golden cage like a queen?

Should we stop looking for perfection and just look for a partner that is good enough?

Can someone who shows up and wants to build a life together be the ultimate turn on?

What's the difference between compromising and settling?

How do you keep the passion alive when you see him every day in his boxers scratching his balding head?

Are soulmates real for some and a myth for others?

Do we sabotage our relationships out of boredom in a relationship?

Can we find ever-lasting love in the casual dating culture?

Can you date someone who identifies as 'poly'?

Would you date a bisexual or is that too much competition?

Are all relationships 'imperfect'?

Can we be happy if we never find 'the one'?

What is 'the future'?

Isn't the present all that counts? So then, isn't the situationship real love?

Note to reader from me:

Would really appreciate a little review on Amazon. If you want me to add some of your questions for my next book, you can add that in the review too.

Thanks for reading!

Scan QR code to access the
Penguin Random House India website